THE GUILTY SECRET

"The Munga tribe had a proverb that said, 'The teeth are smiling, but is the heart?' Inuwa's heart was not smiling. His father did not know the truth. Yes, he had won the feats of skill contest in the initiation rites. But he was not brave. Each boy was required to sleep out in the bush overnight. Inuwa was terrified of the bush after dark, and he had sneaked back into the village and hid in a safe place, slipping back just at dawn.

"Another boy saw him, and he had lied, but the boy seemed to believe him. If the boy knew what really happened and told the judges, he would be disqualified, his ear ring taken away, and he would be disgraced.

"Two tense days passed, and when his father said that Inuwa should be the one to guide him to the hospital, he decided to go. Yet he was afraid. Through unknown bush country! Where wild animals and robbers and goodness knows what else would be waiting for them. . . ."

THE
BRASS
RING

Dorris Blough

The Brethren Press   Elgin, Illinois

THE BRASS RING

Published for The Brethren Press by Pillar Books

Brethren Press edition published October 1975

ISBN: 0–87178–105–0

Printed in the United States of America

The Brethren Press
1451 Dundee Avenue
Elgin, Illinois 60120, U.S.A.

The
Brass
Ring

Chapter 1

TRAPPED!

Inuwa was terrified! The two robbers were so close that he could easily hit them if he tossed a rock. They could not see him because he was screened behind a thick brush covering. He hardly dared breathe. If he started to run away they could easily catch him. He was trapped, and he was scared. More scared than he had ever been in his life. His mouth was dry; he was so tense with fear that he shook. And that made him even more afraid that the two men might hear him.

Thoughts raced through his mind. If only he had not been careless and left the water bottle so that he had had to come back. If only Tursinda were here. That thought took him back to early that morning, when before the sun was up, he and his father had set out on their journey.

What a difficult decision it had been, whether to go on the trip or not. If he stayed he might have to admit to having cheated in the initiation trials. If he went he would face the terrible fear that caused him to cheat in the first place. In agony he had decided he could not face the judges and admit his guilt. It would be easier to escape by being his father's guide to the hospital at Birni. As preparations were made, he was glad to be leaving, but fearful of the trip, and yet excited at the prospect of seeing Birni, the big town that only a couple other boys in the village had ever seen. But he had forgotten about Tursinda, his dog. He would have to leave him behind.

He remembered clearly how, as they started down the path, he gritted his teeth as hard as he could, and the end of the slingshot dug into his hand as he squeezed it so tightly. He did not want to cry!

Then from behind had come one sharp bark. Tursinda

7

did not understand why he was not going along as he always did. That did it. Inuwa shut his eyes tightly. His father could not see the tears, but a boy as big as he did not cry.

Suddenly he had stubbed his toe painfully. Inuwa was glad, for he dropped the guide stick with which he had been leading his father and danced around, yelling, "Ow-w-w!" It was better than crying like a girl.

But his father did not need eyes to understand what was going on.

"Your mother and Ladi will look after Tursinda while you are gone. Don't worry about him."

Tursinda was his very own dog. Everyone had thought the pup was worthless and had given him the name Tursinda, which meant "ignorant." But Inuwa did not care. Wherever he went, Tursinda went; they were inseparable.

He was leaving to walk with his father to the hospital, about eighteen miles from their village. His father had been going blind slowly and now could see only dark and light. The hope was that the doctor could help him.

"Let's get going, son." Mallam Yaga had spoken firmly. "We can't waste much time if we expect to sleep in Uncle Giri's compound tonight. You know I can't walk very fast, so we will just have to keep on the move." His father paused, then added. "You are my eyes, boy. I'm depending on you to get me to the hospital. A boy with a brass ring in his ear can be depended on."

Inuwa turned loose of his trobbing toe. The brass ring in his ear; it was so new he could feel it without touching it. It was truly an honor to wear it, something that should make him very happy. But it was not so.

The Munga tribe had a proverb that said, "The teeth are smiling, but is the heart?" Inuwa's heart was not smiling. His father did not know the truth. Yes, he had won the feats-of-skill contest in the initiation rites, but he was not brave. Each boy was required to sleep out in the bush overnight as part of the bush trials. Inuwa was terrified of the bush after dark, and that night he had sneaked back into the village and hid in a safe place, sneaking back just at dawn. As he had been slipping back at daybreak, another boy had seen him and asked where he was going. He had lied, but the boy seemed to believe him. If the boy figured out what really happened and told the judges Inuwa would be disqualified, his earring taken away, and he would be disgraced.

Two tense days passed, and when his father said that Inuwa should be the one to guide him to the hospital, he decided to go. Yet he was afraid. Through unknown bush country! Where wild animals and robbers and goodness knows what else would be waiting for them! If only Tursinda could have come he would feel safer.

He shook his head. "No, Mama and Ladi will not forget Tursinda." He paused. "He won't let them." He laughed at that, a hollow laugh, but it pushed the lump out of his throat. And they had turned down the path which led away from their village and away from Tursinda.

Inuwa parted the bushes with the utmost care and looked again at his two captors. They were quiet, but alert, their backs to him. He might have to sit here a long time. What would his father do, waiting for him, wondering why he did not return? Inuwa's legs ached from sitting in one position.

As he furtively watched the two men his thoughts returned to the day's journey.

At first the path had been familiar, and they had moved at a fair speed. In spite of his blindness, Mallam Yaga walked tall and straight, a proud man. He tapped his way along with the cane in his right hand. In his left hand he grasped one end of a stick of which Inuwa held the other end. In this way Inuwa could guide his father easily.

On their heads each carried a load. Mallam Yaga's was a huge gourd in which they had placed all the things they would need on the road. There were dishes, a cooking pot, a stirring stick, dried leaves to be cooked, a small packet of salt, a few precious dried tomatoes, matches and a bottle of water. Tied on top of that were two sleeping mats rolled up. Inuwa carried a sack of ground grain for their daily corn mush.

They took only the clothes they were wearing. Inuwa wore a pair of shorts and a *danjiki,* the hand-woven shirt that all boys wore. The shorts were faded and worn, the edges frayed. The shirt was coming apart where the strips

9

Inuwa guided his father on the trail to Birni.

of cloth had been sewed together. He wore these clothes every day, although he had a robe for church and special occasions. Mallam Yaga wore a striped print shirt made by the village tailor. His trousers were of tan cotton. Over these he put a lightweight full-flowing robe of bright blue. It was almost new. Inuwa was barefoot, but Mallam Yaga had sandals made from tires with strips of inner tubes for straps. Each had a small cap which fitted closely. Inuwa's was of white cotton cloth and his father's was made from the same material as his blue robe.

Inuwa had begun to feel a little better as he thought of staying the night with his cousin, Thlama, Uncle Giri's son. They were about the same age and always had fun together.

Inuwa watched familiar landmarks pass and disappear behind them. He did not mind this part of the journey; it was the unknown trail that he dreaded. Yet the farther they went, the farther he was from being found out.

The sun had been well up into the sky and beginning to feel hot on their shoulders when they stopped to ask for a drink of water at a compound near the path. They would not use their own water until they had to. The woman there also gave them something to eat.

It was very hot as they set out again; the sky was cloudless.

By the time the sun was starting down the western half of the sky, they decided they had walked long enough in the heat. They were outside of familiar territory now. Under the shade of a thick *mbula* tree they sat down. Inuwa pulled the water bottle out of the gourd his father had been carrying. It was a krola bottle, a kind of soft drink, with a cornstalk stopper. The water was warm and felt good to their dry throats. Inuwa laid the bottle beside him since they would want more water before they went on. Then they stretched out to rest in the pleasant shade. The slingshot he always carried was placed beside his head. He could not relax, but lay tense, thinking of what lay ahead and behind.

A short time later his father sat up. "Come, Inuwa, it is time to go. Did you fall asleep?"

"Yes, I think so," he lied, and yawned. "How much farther to Uncle Giri's compound?"

11

"We should get there in time to eat with them, just about dark."

That seemed like a very long time to Inuwa, especially since his stomach was already beginning to complain about being empty. But he said nothing.

He hopped up quickly, picked up his slingshot and reached for the sack of grain he had been carrying. He put it into his father's hands.

"You carry the grain this time, Baba. I'll carry the other things."

Mallam Yaga took the sack and placed it on his own head then waited for Inuwa. Inuwa stooped and carefully lifted the gourd. It was heavy, but he managed to get it onto his head. Then he bent his knees slowly to reach for the guide stick. He touched his father's hand with it, and his father grasped his end of it. They were off down the path again.

Inuwa's attention had snapped back to the present as one of the men stood up cautiously and peered in the direction from which Inuwa had come. The man shook his head silently and sat down again.

Inuwa just had to move his stiffened left leg. He did it slowly and without a sound. The late afternoon heat was stifling here where there was no breeze. He wished for another drink, but that was impossible. His thirst took him back to the afternoon's events that had resulted in the trap he was in.

He and his father had walked steadily. The sweat trickled down their faces. It tickled at first; then it became annoying. Inuwa was thirsty again.

If only he did not have to keep hold of the guide stick all the time he could shoot at things with his slingshot. He never went anyplace without his sling and was always aiming at something or other. As a result he was the best shot in the village. It was at least something to do to watch for targets along the way and think just how he would make the shot if he could. He did stop now and then to pick up a stone that looked just right.

It was his skill with the slingshot that had made it possible for him to be one of the youngest members of the

Munga tribe ever to go through the initiation ceremonies. Boys could begin taking part in the contests when they were about ten years old, but few passed before they were at least fourteen. No one had written down his birthday, but he had been born the year of the flood on the Gongola River, which had been twelve years ago.

Inuwa had bested all the competing boys, both in total score when shooting at a target and in number of birds killed in the allotted time. Again he sensed rather than felt the brass ring in his ear. He did not deserve it; he should still be wearing the wire ring that all boys wore. Perhaps he could make up for it by working extra hard in school so that no one would think to question the brass ring. Yes, that's what he would do. There were six weeks of vacation and then he would begin the seventh grade in the school in Turwa. Oh, how hard he would work! Then his heart could smile too.

Inuwa and his father had walked on and on, not talking. The path was monotonous. He was glad his sister had not come. Girls could not take walking so far in the heat without water.

Their shadows lengthened. The sun was halfway to the horizon.

Oh, how he had wished for a drink! He knew that they carried only a small amount of water, and there were not many places to find water along the way. They would have to make the water stretch. But, oh, he was thirsty!

Staring at the men through the bushes, Inuwa remembered very well what had happened next. He had looked ahead up the path. It ran straight for quite some distance and then branched off to the right. There was a large tree where the path made its turn. He would make himself wait until there to ask for a drink.

It seemed to Inuwa that the distance to the tree became longer instead of shorter. To take his mind off his thirst, he looked about across the countryside. There was no spring or river near, so there were no compounds, homes where people lived, for miles in any direction. This was called bush country because it was well covered with short bushes and stunted trees. In rainy season the ground was covered with green grass, but now there was not a sprig to be seen. The ground was brown and mostly barren. But over there was a "crazy" tree. It had no leaves in the rainy season but put out its leaves during the dry season. So people called it crazy. Here and there on the ground grew clumps of shiny leaves, a bright, bright green. They cheered the landscape.

The horizon was hazy from the *harmattan,* the fine dust which sifted down from the Sahara desert. If the dust were heavy enough it would keep the hot sun's rays from reaching the earth, and it would be cooler. But there was not enough to do that today.

Inuwa looked up the path again. The tree was not far away anymore. He gave a little tug on the guide stick as he hurried faster.

"What is it, Inuwa? Why the hurry?" asked his father.

"There is a big tree where we can stop for a drink. And am I thirsty!"

When they reached the tree, Inuwa carefully set down the gourd from his own head and then helped to take the sack from off his father's. Then he dropped to the ground in the cool shade and reached for the bottle of water among the items in the gourd. It wasn't there!

Then he remembered. He had laid it down beside him, thinking they would take another drink before they started again, and he had left it.

"Baba! The bottle of water . . . I . . . I left it back where we stopped to rest!"

"Son, we can't go on without water!" Mallam Yaga paused, considering. "Even if we could find water we have no bottle to carry it in. I'm afraid you will have to go back after it."

"But it is getting late."

"Yes, that means you must hurry. It is still closer back to the water than on to Uncle Giri's. I will wait right here. You should not run in this heat when you are already thirsty. Walk quickly. Drink a little of the water when you get there, some more on the way, but not all. It can't be too far to Uncle Giri's compound from here, but we must not run out of water completely."

Mallam Yaga reached deep down into the pocket of his robe and brought out a mango. "Here is something that should help a little. I was saving this for some special time. I guess this is it."

"*Aiya mana!*" Inuwa took a bite of the luscious bright

14

yellow fruit. He swallowed the sweet moisture. He hesitated wondering what to say. He was afraid to go back alone. "Baba, will you be all right here? You remember the warning about thieves on this path. Someone was robbed just this week. Maybe we should just push on and hope to reach . . ."

"I will be all right. Put the grain and the gourd behind some bushes."

Inuwa did it reluctantly.

"Do you have your slingshot?" his father asked.

"Of course. I will hurry, Baba."

"Good-bye, son."

"Good-bye," Inuwa said with a cheerfulness he did not feel.

He set off at a fast clip, munching on his mango as he went. He was not as thirsty anymore, although the sun was still very hot.

The sun was dropping, rapidly it seemed. He did not want to be alone after dark! The thought added speed to his feet. He was so very tired and thirsty when he finally recognized certain trees and rocks that told him he was close to the spot where they had rested. Yes, he saw the *mbula* tree up ahead. If only the water bottle was still there.

He ran the last little way and eagerly searched the spot where they had stopped. It was there! It had rolled under a clump of the bright leaves.

He would take a drink and rest just a minute or two. He sat down behind a big clump of bushes in complete shade and drank just a little water. It felt good going down his throat. One more sip and he would be on his way again. He would run. They had to reach Uncle Giri's compound. He could not sleep in the bush!

Then it happened. Suddenly he heard voices. He did not move but watched eagerly through his screen of bushes. Two men came into the small clearing and looked around furtively. Then they crawled behind another clump of bushes only a short distance from where Inuwa was sitting. They acted as if they were hiding. Why would they do that? They began to speak in low voices, but Inuwa could hear them.

"They were to start from Gombe this morning which

15

means they should be coming along here before long," said one of the men.

The other asked, "Do you suppose they will be carrying as much as two hundred pounds in cash?"

"More than that," the other replied. "It must be enough to pay the teachers at Turwa and Belma."

Thieves! They were thieves! If he moved they would discover him. If he did not leave soon darkness would fall before he could find his way back to his father, blind and alone in the bush. What was he going to do?

Chapter 2

A HYENA LAUGHS

Now his right leg cried out to be moved. Slowly, slowly Inuwa changed his position, never taking his eyes off the two men who unknowingly held him captive. He thought of his father, waiting for him. As soon as the sun went down, it would be dark. The path would be difficult to find unless there was a moon. He might get lost!

The men went on talking in low tones.

"They may come by at any time now, so this is what we will do. They usually travel two together, sometimes three, to carry the money. Since there are only two of us, we will have to play it smart. They will be facing us. We will pretend that there is a third man behind them. Let's call him Musa. We will keep talking to him. That will fool them."

"*I'i*, that's a good trick," agreed the other man.

He had taken his knife from its arm scabbard and was fingering it. The thin sharp edge shone in the late afternoon sun. Inuwa shivered. This was no man to mess with. Even a slingshot would be of little use here.

The other man was holding a homemade Dane gun. He brought it to his shoulder, aimed at an imaginary spot on the road and sighted it. It would not be very accurate at a distance, but during a robbery it would be deadly.

Inuwa wished all the more that he were safely away from this place. But he might have to stay for hours yet. His legs ached again, and he was still thirsty. He held the water bottle in one hand. Just in case he saw a chance to run, he did not want to leave the thing that had brought him back here.

He did not take his eyes off the two men.

Suddenly he saw movement out of the corner of his eye. He carefully moved only his head to see what it was. There, only about three long steps from him was a *katanga,*

17

a deadly little snake, not much longer than his arm. And it was coming toward him. What should he do? If he moved they would find him. If he did not the snake would bite.

Inuwa had to clamp his teeth together to keep from making a noise. His hand ached from gripping the water bottle to keep himself from moving. He could kill the snake with his slingshot, but then the men would find him.

The snake stopped, crawled a little further, stopped again. It was obviously not looking for humans. A small bird was on the ground very close to Inuwa. With the hand that was out of sight of the snake, Inuwa scared the bird away. Then the snake abruptly turned and started slowly away. Inuwa relaxed his tired jaws.

Now the snake was crawling on a collision path with the two men, but their backs were to it. If they turned and saw it they would shoot it with their gun or throw the sharp knife at it. But if they did not the snake just might possibly bite one of them.

Inuwa watched through the leaves of his hiding place, fascinated. The snake moved slowly on, looking for food. The two men were quiet, waiting, unaware that the snake was near. Now it was a man's length away from the men.

If the snake heard or saw the men it would run away because most snakes do not attack humans unless they are cornered. But if it should run into them then it would act to protect itself.

The snake moved on. Now it was only an arm's length away.

Inuwa tensed his muscles ready to leap. He would have to act faster than he had ever done in his life. Something was going to happen very soon.

Suddenly the big man saw the snake. He yelled, "Look out!"

That was all Inuwa heard. He was gone, flying down the path as if a devil were after him. He did not even slow up until he could absolutely run no longer and had to catch his breath. Even to do that he ran off beside the path and hid behind some bushes.

As soon as he could breathe normally again, he listened for sounds of someone coming after him, but there were none.

He set off again at a fast trot, a speed he knew he could

maintain for a considerable length of time. He took a sip of the water as he ran.

On and on he sped.

Ahead of him was a huge pile of rocks. He remembered that the path veered around them. Suddenly as he made the turn, he was face to face with three men. One carried a gun. Inuwa was so surprised and so scared he could not say a word. He halted abruptly and just stared.

"Look out there!" cried one of the men. "Why the hurry?"

Another man said, "Say, aren't you Mallam Yaga's son from Turwa?"

Inuwa nodded in sudden relief; he recognized the speaker. His quick gaze took in the gun and the box one man was carrying. The men with the money!

His tongue was suddenly freed. "There are two robbers up the road! Waiting for you! I was hiding in the bushes and got away when a snake scared them. You'd better not go this way."

The men looked uneasily at each other.

Inuwa went on. "But I heard them talking." Quickly he told them of the conversation he had overheard.

"I know what we can do," said one of the men. "Musa, since you have the gun you go over in the bushes and follow just far enough behind to keep us in sight. Then you will be in a position to upset their plans."

"Is his name really Musa?" asked Inuwa.

The man nodded.

Inuwa laughed. "Those men are going to be poisoned by their own medicine."

Inuwa started on down the path. "I hope you make it through all right."

"Thanks for the help, boy. You may have saved us," called one of the men as they turned to go.

Inuwa was still chuckling as he ran. He almost wished he could be there to see how surprised those two men would be.

The sun went down and would be followed almost immediately by darkness. Inuwa ran with his heart in his throat. He didn't want to be alone in the dark!

There was almost no light when Inuwa reached the place

where he had left his father. He called softly, "Baba, where are you?"

"Here, son," came the answer. Inuwa followed the voice.

"I was getting worried. What happened?"

Inuwa's words tumbled over each other as he told about his escape.

His father put his hand on Inuwa's. "That was dangerous, but you used your head."

"But we can't get to Uncle Giri's compound now, can we?"

"No, we will have to sleep out here tonight."

Inuwa was glad his father could not see the fear he could not hide.

"What will we do for food?" asked Inuwa. "There is a great big hole in my stomach."

"We have no water in which to cook our guinea corn for mush, and we really wouldn't want to build a fire that might attract those robbers. So it looks like we sleep on empty stomachs tonight."

"*Aiya*," sighed Inuwa. "I'm not sure I'll sleep at all out here." Then he added quickly, ". . . 'cause I'm so hungry."

"Maybe this will help," said his father. And he pulled out two more mangoes from deep in his huge robe pocket.

"*Wana, wana, wana,* Baba," cried Inuwa and immediately sank his teeth into the sweet fruit.

"Eat it quickly. You must find a good place to put down our sleeping mats before it gets any darker."

Inuwa nodded and went off munching on the mango, warily watching the brush on all sides. Instantly he remembered the instructions about choosing a place to sleep in the bush that he had received the night of the bush trials.

Soon he was back to lead his father to a spot not far away. It was protected on three sides by bushes. First, with a branch off a bush, Inuwa swept it clear of sticks and leaves that might hide snakes. Then he unrolled the sleeping mats and laid them down side by side. The sack of grain and the gourd had to be put in a protected place. Then he helped his father to his sleeping mat. Finally he placed his slingshot and five good stones right beside his grass mat.

Inuwa lay down on his mat but with no thought of sleep. Very quickly he heard the even breathing of his father, indicating sleep. If only he could be as fearless as his father. Inuwa could not remember when his father hesitated to do something that needed to be done. Inuwa thought, "Even if they can't cure his blindness he will not let it conquer him. He will prove somehow that he is stronger than it." It was time to sleep, so his father slept, without fear. And Inuwa was tired, very tired, but his body remained tense, listening to the night sounds. He was not brave! He could not even pretend to be.

He stared at the stars, which seemed so near yet not a part of his world. His world was real all around him, animals calling, stealthy steps, movements he could only hear, not see. How could he go on tomorrow with no rest tonight?

Once he sat up quickly, but it was only an owl. What if the owl were chasing a snake? Inuwa held his breath and listened to catch the noise of the snake slipping along on its belly. The pale moon rising low in the east turned the world into dim shapes and dimmer shadows. He lay back down, tense and ready. And he was so tired.

Suddenly he was awakened by his father shaking him but saying nothing. It was a still night with the moon starting to descend the western sky. Inuwa's heart leaped to his throat, but he said very quietly, "What is it?"

"Listen," warned his father.

They both clearly heard the sniffing of an animal. It was just on the other side of the bushes that surrounded them. But the bushes were no real protection from wild animals. Was it a leopard, a wild pig, an antelope?

Suddenly they both leaped to their feet as the hideous laugh of a hyena rang through the night air right beside them.

Chapter 3

MINDI!

"Baba," whispered Inuwa, "do you think the hyena is after us?"

"Hyenas have been known to attack people," replied his father. "I have my knife ready."

"But you can't see!"

"I'll do what I can."

Inuwa looked around him. It was really not dark. The moon was lopsided but bright. He could clearly see the bushes, the mats, the slingshot in his hand. He had grabbed it as he jumped up.

Where was that hyena now? Did he know they were there? The gentle breeze was blowing their scent away from the hyena.

Inuwa fitted a stone into the slingshot and turned around slowly, peering through the bushes. Then he heard a slight noise there, where the hyena had been before. He was still there!

Suddenly the moonlight shone on two round eyes that could be seen through an opening in the bushes. Without waiting a split second, Inuwa raised his sling and let a rock fly with all the strength he had. It was immediately followed by a yelp of pain, and the eyes disappeared. Then they heard the loping gait of the animal as he took off through the bushes.

"Is he leaving? What made him yelp?"

"I hit him with a stone from my sling, right in the eye, I think."

"Good shot!"

Suddenly Inuwa's legs became like young henna stems, hardly able to hold him up. What if his father hadn't wakened? What if the hyena . . . a shiver shook his body.

Anxiously, Inuwa asked, "What do we do now?"

22

"Surely there are no robbers out this time of night. We will build a small fire."

"I couldn't sleep any more tonight," said Inuwa.

"Me either," said his father. "We will sit by the fire until morning."

With one of their precious matches, Inuwa built a small fire. They sat down beside it, Inuwa feeding sticks to it. The leaping blaze was reassuring, but he kept watch and listened intently.

"I didn't mean to fall asleep, Baba. What made you wake up?"

"I am a light sleeper, but I'm not sure exactly what wakened me. Some different noise, I guess. If only I could see!"

Though his father was of a strong build, Inuwa thought he seemed small as his almost sightless eyes stared dejectedly at the flames.

"Do you know why you went blind?"

"No, things just began to get hazy, then dim, and finally I could see nothing except light and darkness."

"Do you really think you can get help at the hospital?"

"People say there is a white *dokita* there who can make my eyes see again."

"And if he can't?" asked Inuwa softly.

"Then you will guide me all the way back home, and I will be a blind man the rest of my life."

"But I can plant the farm and hoe it. Can't I?"

"Yes, son, but you forget that you are in school much of the time. I want you to become a teacher someday. No, I want to use my own eyes. If God wills, I will see again."

"Wouldn't Mama be surprised if she saw you coming home without your stick and without me leading you? Wouldn't that be wonderful?"

"Yes, that would really be wonderful!" His father pulled his shoulders back, and his face lost the dejected look as he smiled.

Inuwa sat staring into the fire for a long time, listening to the night sounds around him. Somehow they were less scary with the fire crackling merrily. And his father's calm presence was reassuring. He thought of Tursinda. He had never been afraid with Tursinda by his side. He had made Ladi promise to keep Tursinda away from Mama Wani's part of the compound. She was his father's second wife, and she did not like dogs, not a bit, particularly Tursinda. The dog had always slept beside Inuwa on his mat. Where would he be sleeping now? The thought was too painful. He shook his head and looked up at the sky. The funny lopsided moon was going down the western side as the eastern sky began to brighten and faded out the moon's soft glow.

Inuwa stood up.

"Time to get started, Baba. Perhaps we will reach Uncle Giri's house before it gets too hot. Am I ever hungry! Did you just happen to hide more mangoes in your robe?"

Mallam Yaga reached deep into his robe pocket, his hand searching for that which was hidden there.

"No, but look what I did find." He brought out four peanut sticks, hard, crunchy and delicious.

"*Aiya!* you thought of everything!"

"Let's eat these, drink some water and be on our way."

They divided the water that was left. Inuwa put the gourd on his father's head and took the sack of grain on his own. With his sling held ready in his left hand, he found his way back to the path, his right hand holding the guide stick for his father.

As soon as the sun peeked above the horizon, they knew it would be a miserably hot day. They walked quickly in the still morning while it was yet cool. How good it was to be in the daylight. He never wanted to stay out in the bush again, never! He brought up his sling with his left hand and pretended to be aiming at the hyena. A shiver went through him as he thought of how the story might have ended.

Animals were out looking for food before the heat was upon them. Cottontail rabbits ran at their approach. He would have tried to kill one, but dressing it would delay them. Wild guinea fowls flew down from a leafless tree and chattered off together to look for food. Once an awkward old hornbill waddled across the path ahead. No one was afraid with the hornbill near. He was a sign that all was well in the bush. How nice it would have been to bring Tursinda. What fun they would have had chasing the funny fat little mice that appeared at the mouths of their holes now and then. Inuwa recognized a pair of parakeets and several other birds giving their warning cry at the approach of the two humans.

24

They walked and walked. Sweat poured from both of them. The terrain was going down little by little. At mid-morning the path veered abruptly to the left.

"We have changed direction, haven't we?" asked Mallam Yaga.

"Yes, we are going more toward the east now," replied Inuwa.

"Then it is not so much farther," said his father.

"That peanut stick didn't last very long. I hope they have chicken *panya* at Uncle Giri's. I'm terribly hungry."

"Chicken *panya* does sound good. But they don't know we are coming, so don't get your hopes up."

They walked on in silence. Abruptly they came to the top of a small hill where a little valley stretched before them. Inuwa stopped.

"What is it?" asked his father.

"We are at the top of a rise and I can see a long way."

"Then we are very close to the village of Ghong. Do you see the smoke from a compound directly in front of you?"

"Yes," replied Inuwa. "It is a big compound. I can see into it. There are many people. Do lots of people live in Uncle Giri's compound?"

"No, not so many, just my brother, Giri, and his wife and the four children."

"Well, there certainly are . . ." but he stopped. The people in the compound suddenly began moving. Most of them seemed to be running out of the gate. And then the noise reached their ears.

Mallam Yaga exclaimed, "Someone has died! Listen to the crying. Where is it coming from?"

"From Uncle Giri's compound," replied Inuwa.

"Oh, no! Who has died?"

"What shall we do?" asked Inuwa.

"We won't find out standing here. Let's go on," said his father gravely.

Inuwa picked his way down the rocky path. His stomach growled at him. Maybe he should not think of himself at a time like this, but if someone had just died he was not likely to get anything to eat for a long time. At the bottom of the hill, Inuwa led the way toward the compound. They approached the group of people standing near the compound gatehouse. There were only a few, the others having scattered in all directions. They were busily talking among themselves, gesturing excitedly, pointing to the compound.

Suddenly out of the gatehouse came a woman wearing only an old cloth wrapped around her. She gave out an ear-piercing shriek, put her hand over her mouth and began to dance around the group, screaming as she went.

One of the people, a young man, turned and saw Inuwa and his father approaching. He pointed toward them and said something to the others. Then he started running toward them. A short distance away, he stopped and called, "Don't come any closer!"

"Why?"

"*Mindi!* A child has just died of *mindi!*"

Mindi! The deadly meningitis. And who had died?

Chapter 4

LOST IN THE BUSH

"*Mindi!*" echoed Mallam Yaga.

"Baba, do . . . do you suppose it could be one of my cousins, maybe even Thlama?" asked Inuwa.

Mallam Yaga spoke quickly to the boy who had come to meet them. "Who is it who died? Someone in Mallam Giri's compound?"

"Yes . . ." began the boy.

"Was it Thlama?" Inuwa asked quickly.

"No, it was the baby, just born last rainy season. It hadn't been well for some time and then this happened."

"I must go to my brother. If it had to happen I am glad I came today," said Mallam Yaga.

"Oh, is he your brother?" said the boy. "Then you are Mallam Yaga from Turwa."

"Yes," nodded Inuwa's father. "I must see him."

Again it came to Inuwa's mind, "He's not afraid to do anything if he thinks it is the right thing to do."

The boy turned and started toward the compound. Inuwa and his father followed as quickly as they could with Mallam Yaga tapping his way along.

As they passed the woman who was dancing and crying, Inuwa asked the young man, "Who is that?"

"She is the baby's grandmother, mother of Mallam Giri's wife."

They made their way through the outside door of the small round gatehouse, through the house and out the door which led into the compound.

People were still milling around, crying. All the women had taken off their headscarves as a sign of mourning. Through an open door Inuwa could see the women who were wrapping the body for burial. He recognized his own

27

kaka, Jeto, his father's mother, among them, but she did not see him.

A cluster of men around the door of a certain house showed where they would find Mallam Giri. The boy who was leading them pointed there. Inuwa led his father to the group and quickly moved away.

Children were usually sent somewhere else during a time like this. Inuwa did not want to be around. Where could he find Thlama? He ran after the boy who had brought them and caught up with him as he was going out the gatehouse. "Do you know where Thlama is?"

"I'm not sure, but I would guess he is at his *kaka*'s house. Do you know where that is?"

Inuwa said he thought he could find it and ran off in the direction he remembered going to his grandmother's house the last time he had visited here. They had not come often because it was a day's long walk, but he had been there last dry season.

He passed a group of men digging a hole in the ground. When babies died, they were usually buried near the compound in a corn field. There would not be a big funeral since this was such a small child. Inuwa wondered how long they would stay here now that this had happened.

His *kaka*'s compound was not far. When he reached it, he walked right in and called, "Thlama."

From behind a grass mat that shielded the cooking house stepped a young boy with a dog at his heels. Inuwa was startled for just a moment.

"Thlama! You are so tall!"

"Look who is talking. So are you."

They both laughed.

Then Thlama noted the earring in Inuwa's ear. "You passed your test! But you aren't any older than I am!"

Inuwa nodded but glanced away quickly.

Thalma went on. "A brass ring! *Aiya*, good, good, good! You will have to tell me about it."

"I will . . . when we have time," replied Inuwa.

"I didn't know you were coming, Inuwa. When did you get here?"

"Just now, in time to hear the crying begin. I'm sorry . . . about the baby."

Thalma turned away, quick tears starting in his eyes.

28

"They were sure early this morning that the baby wouldn't live, so I came over here. I hope no one else gets *mindi*."

Inuwa nodded solemnly.

"How long can you stay?" asked Thlama.

"I don't know. We are on the way to the hospital at Birni. But now that this has happened, I'm sure Baba will want to stay a while."

"Say, that's fine! We've got the best swimming hole you ever saw. Want to go right now?"

"Well . . ." Inuwa hesitated. "I ran into robbers last night."

"Robbers!" shouted Thlama. "*Aiya*! Tell me about it! Hey, Dawuda, come listen to this. He ran into robbers last night!"

Another boy about their age came from behind the cooking shelter on the run. A girl, a little younger than they, came too.

"Dawuda lives in the compound right beside ours. We play together," explained Thlama. Then he turned to the girl. "Saratu, who asked you?" To Inuwa he said, "She lives in that compound over there." He pointed.

The girl smiled a shy smile and said, "I'd like to hear about it too."

"This isn't for girls," said Thlama roughly.

"Let her stay; it's all right," said Inuwa. He noted that she had a cloth wrapped around one leg.

"You'll be sorry. She's a pest," was Thlama's comment.

"Tell us about the robbers!" urged Dawuda.

"I'd rather have something to eat. I started to say that the robbers kept us from getting here last night, and all I've had to eat today was two peanut sticks early this morning."

"That's no problem. We've got food. Hey, Alisu," he called out in the direction of the cooking house, "get some food for Inuwa. He and Uncle Yaga came all the way from Turwa, and he's hungry."

"I'll get it," said Saratu eagerly.

Soon Inuwa was sitting in front of a dish of guinea corn mush and *panya*. And it was chicken *panya*! He broke off a piece of the mush and dipped it into the chicken broth, then popped it into his mouth. Did that ever taste good! Saratu had moved much closer and was watching Inuwa's every move.

"Saratu! Go away!" ordered Thlama.

She slid backward just a little.

"Can't you tell us about the robbers while you eat?" asked Dawuda.

Inuwa shook his head without stopping to reply. So the other two boys told all the things they had heard about robbers recently, the stories getting bigger as they talked. Inuwa kept on eating. Saratu inched closer again.

Finally, when he could eat no more, he wiped his fingers on his shorts and leaned back against the mud storage bin behind him.

Thlama noticed Saratu again. "Saratu, this isn't for girls!" She scooted back.

The children waited expectantly. Even the dog was listening.

Inuwa told the story slowly and in great detail, clearly enjoying his audience. When he described how he raced off when the man yelled, the others clapped their hands gleefully.

When he was finished, the children's eyes were wide.

"Aren't you afraid to go back home that way?" asked Saratu breathlessly.

Inuwa shrugged his shoulders. "There isn't any other path, so I guess we will. But maybe Baba will be able to see when we go back home. That would help."

"Does he really think the white *dokita* can make him see?" asked Thlama.

"He doesn't know for sure. But I hope we aren't making this long trip *gapani*."

Dawuda wiped the sweat from his face. "It is so hot that I can think of nothing more important than showing Inuwa our swimming place. Come on."

No one waited for a second suggestion as the boys jumped to their feet.

As they started out of the compound, Thlama turned to Saratu who appeared to be following them. "Saratu, you absolutely cannot go swimming. Go on home!" She turned back but watched them go.

Thlama led the way as they followed a path between compounds to the edge of the village. Then they chose a trail from the several there and headed for a group of trees not far away. The dog followed closely at their heels.

*Inuwa, Thlama, and Dawuda found a water hole
in the trees.*

"The water hole is there in those trees," explained Dawuda.

"Say, you don't have to go very far, do you?" said Inuwa.

As they neared the trees, each boy took off his shirt. At the edge they kicked off their trousers and ran the last few steps to plunge into the cool water.

Some time later the three boys walked slowly back to the village. Just as they reached their grandmother's compound, Saratu came around the corner.

"What are you going to do now?" she asked.

They did not answer.

"Can I play too?"

"Go away," commanded Thlama crossly.

"Girls!" said Dawuda.

Lack of sleep and strenuous activity had left Inuwa very tired. He lay down on a mat in one of the sleeping houses and dropped into the sleep of fatigue.

When he awoke some time later, his father was there. Inuwa's first thought was food. "Did you ever get anything to eat, Baba?"

"Yes. While they were digging the grave for the baby someone brought me food. They buried the baby about noon."

"How long will we stay here?" asked Inuwa.

"I can't run off quickly after this tragedy. I suppose we can move on day after tomorrow."

"Baba, can I stay here in this compound with Thlama?"

"I imagine Thlama will remain here until his mother feels a little better. She is taking it very hard. You might as well be here too. I will talk with *Kaka* Jeto about it."

The sun poured down on the earth with no *harmattan* or clouds to stop its rays. In the cool of the mud-walled house Inuwa and Thlama sat and talked. Thlama insisted on hearing about the initiation contests.

"Tell me how you won your brass ring," urged Thlama. "Was it in the bush trials or the skills contests?" Without waiting for a reply, he went on. "I'll bet it was in the bush trials. Of course, you were better than any of the boys at taking care of yourself in the bush."

Inuwa shook his head, not daring to look at Thlama. Surely anyone could see the lie in his eyes.

Quickly he reached over and picked up his slingshot. "No, I shot further and more accurately than anybody else."

Thlama looked surprised. "But how about the bush trials? If you would escape from the robbers and chase away the hyena, you surely . . ."

Inuwa sought frantically for some way to change the subject. How could he tell Thlama how terrified he had been, afraid to go to sleep, afraid to go alone along the trail, afraid to let his father sense his fear?

Suddenly he thought of something. Picking up his sling as he rose to his feet, he said, "Let's go find a shady spot and shoot at a target."

"Good," responded Thlama. "You can show me how to do it. Maybe I can win my brass ring next year."

The next day they played a ball game in which they could touch the ball only with their feet. They tried to make a goal by kicking the ball between two grain bins. Saratu begged to play, but Thlama and Dawuda refused. Thlama's dog, Yaro, loved to catch the ball and run off with it, making them chase him. Finally they gave up and decided to play ball with Yaro.

And they made preparations for the next day's journey. Inuwa's grandmother fried a batch of peanut sticks and little bean cakes that Inuwa declared tasted better than any he had ever eaten. Mallam Yaga replenished his supply of mangoes. They bought a packet of sweet biscuits from a trader, and Inuwa was allowed to buy something special, wrapped candies, two for a *kobo*, one-cent piece. His father let him buy six. Inuwa hid them carefully in his pocket.

On the morning of the following day Inuwa wakened early and lay there thinking. If only he could stay with Thlama and not have to go on. He had had enough of the bush. He did not want to have to face any more hyenas or robbers. But who would go with his father?

It was almost daylight; the roosters were crowing. He could hear people moving around outside. They were to leave as soon as possible. He heard his father stirring, so he got up and began rolling up his own sleeping mat. He helped his father with his and they went outside.

In the predawn glow Kaka Jeto served them guinea corn mush. She was a little wrinkled woman who smiled easily. Inuwa was sorry she had been gone from her compound so much while he was there. She always made him feel different than his parents did, more important somehow.

Now, as they were ready to leave, she came to him. Into his hand she pressed a shilling. "You buy yourself something special when you get to the big market at Birni," she said. "That will help you forget about missing Tursinda."

She even understood about his dog. Inuwa wished they did not live so far from this wonderful grandmother.

As they were eating, Uncle Giri came. Inuwa moved away so Uncle Giri and his father could talk. In just a few minutes Uncle Giri left and his father called Inuwa to him. "Uncle Giri wanted to know if it was all right for someone to travel with us to the hospital. The person has a bad leg ulcer and needs to see the *dokita*. I told him it was all right."

Inuwa agreed quickly. Here was his chance! His father would not need him. "Baba . . ." he began.

"Is everything ready, Inuwa? We need to be on our way."

His courage failed him, and he turned to check again that everything was in the gourd. It would be heavier this time with the things his grandmother had added. He carried the gourd to the door of the gatehouse and set it down. He stood thinking briefly then turned to go back to his father. "I must tell him I want to stay here," he thought.

Just then Saratu came dashing through the gatehouse. She almost ran into Inuwa. Suddenly her exuberance was gone and she was embarrassed and shy again.

"Hello, Inuwa," she said softly.

Inuwa rather liked Saratu. "We will be leaving very soon," he said. "We should be in Birni tomorrow night." It was certainly not likely that Saratu would be going to the big city for a long time. It was something to brag about.

She nodded and smiled. "Isn't it wonderful?"

Inuwa looked at her sharply. She had said that in a strange way.

34

His father called to him. "Come, Inuwa, let's see that we have everything."

Inuwa turned and ran back to the house where he and his father had been sleeping. He must tell his father. "I've already checked the gourd; it's all there." He stopped, then went on. "Baba . . ." He paused. Then suddenly he knew he could not bring himself to tell his father he did not want to go. His father would ask why, and the answer would be detected in his voice—fear. His father would hear it. Inuwa lifted the sack of grain to his father's head and led him to where the gourd sat.

As they reached the gatehouse a tall man walked through the door. He said to Inuwa, "Your fellow traveler is ready. Are you?"

Inuwa looked at the man's legs, expecting to see a bandaged sore. There was none. His gaze moved to Saratu who now stood beside the man. He stared at her and then slowly it dawned on him.

"You mean . . . you?" he faltered.

Saratu nodded. "This is my father."

Inuwa was too dazed to say any more. He reached down to pick up the gourd. Saratu quickly stepped over and helped set it on his head. He could not even manage to say thanks.

Saratu's father turned around and picked up a gourd piled high with things. He set it on Saratu's head. It held almost as many items as Inuwa's. Inuwa had to grudgingly admit that she had to be strong to carry all that.

They had already said their thanks and good-byes to the people of his grandmother's compound. Thlama came running from where he had been carrying water.

Kaka Jeto had gone after a last-minute item and came now. She slipped something into Inuwa's gourd and another into Saratu's.

"Saratu is almost like one of my children, Yaga," his grandmother said. "I hate to see her go on this long trek, but you will be glad she went. She can cook for all of you at the hospital."

"Well," thought Inuwa, "maybe there is some good in her going after all." Inuwa did not like to cook.

They were to stay with friends that night. "Be sure to

greet Mallam Birama and his wife for me," said Kaka Jeto. They all waved farewell.

The sun was just showing itself above the horizon as they started down the path. Soon it joined a bigger road, obviously well traveled, and they turned toward Birni, away from Turwa. As Inuwa looked out across the bush country ahead, he was suddenly excited. He was going to Birni! Only a couple of other boys in his village had ever been to the big city. Their stories had made him curious. Now he was going to see for himself. This step toward Birni, away from Turwa, gave him a feeling of freedom—freedom from the possibility of being found out. There was still the gnawing, guilty feeling in his stomach. He had thought it would disappear when Turwa was out of sight, but in Birni he would be free! He could forget it all in exciting, wonderful Birni.

They set out in single file. Inuwa and his father led, followed by Saratu. They walked slowly but steadily for what seemed a long time to Inuwa. Soon after they started, the *harmattan* had begun to drift in, so the morning was not hot.

Inuwa's grandmother had washed his shorts and shirt as well as the clothes his father was wearing. She had not repaired the rips, but Inuwa was not aware of them anyway. Saratu's *luptu* was a short dress made of a flowered print. Her *zhebi,* a long piece of cloth with a geometrical design in olive and orange, was wrapped around and fastened at the waist. As did every girl, she wore a headscarf around her head and tied at the nape of her neck. The design was of birds in blue and pink. She was barefoot.

Just below the knee of her left leg a bandage covered a large ulcer. It had started long ago, growing from a tiny mosquito bite to an open sore. It would get better and then worse until now nothing seemed to help anymore.

Inuwa grew tired of having to hold his body so straight and his right arm in a fixed position. He would like to have suggested a rest stop, but he was not about to be the first to mention it. Finally, it was Mallam Yaga who indicated a need to rest.

They sat down in the shade of a tree and took little drinks of water several times rather than much immediately. Saratu timidly sat down near Inuwa.

"Shall we see what your grandmother gave us?" she asked.

With a nod, Inuwa reached into his gourd. He pulled out a shiny white piece of taffy. Saratu found hers too. Saratu grinned. "Kaka Jeto knows I save my money to buy taffy."

They munched in silence.

"How long have you had trouble with your leg?" Mallam Yaga asked.

"For several years," Saratu replied. "If I waited much longer the sore would be down to the bone and then it would be too late. They say there is good medicine at the hospital in Birni. I am so glad that you let me walk with you since I must go slowly too."

"We are glad for your company, Saratu. Right, Inuwa?"

Inuwa was suddenly embarrassed. "Uh . . . yes." But his stumbling made him sound unconvincing. Then he was even more embarrassed.

Saratu said quickly, "When do you think we will reach Birni, Mallam Yaga?"

As they talked, Inuwa let his mind wander back to Tursinda again. Would they really look after him, or would he have to go scavenge for his food like many of the other village dogs? He would go without some of his food to give to Tursinda. But he was sure Ladi would not do that. If Tursinda had been with him out in the bush he would not have been afraid.

Inuwa jumped to his feet. He wanted to be under way. Whatever Inuwa did, Saratu did. She jumped up too.

At food time they stopped again. They ate the peanut sticks and bean cakes that Kaka Jeto had sent. Saratu also had food prepared.

The *harmattan* dust had become heavier and heavier through the morning. They needed no shade for protection from the sun. It was even cooler than when they started. They should make good time today.

Shortly after they started on again, they came to a place where the road divided.

"Your father said we could go either way at this junction, Saratu," said Mallam Yaga, "but he said the left path is a short-cut."

"That is the one for us then," said Inuwa.

And they moved slowly down the left trail. They walked

on and on. This trail was not as distinct as the other had been. Inuwa was beginning to get very tired, and he noted that Saratu was limping. But he could not ask them to stop.

Saratu called out. "I'm tired. Let's stop and rest." Girls were surely different. Saratu was not ashamed to admit she was tired.

They all stretched out for a nap. Inuwa could not go to sleep. What would Tursinda do all day with no one to chase rats with or race with? He made himself think of the trail ahead, but that was not pleasant either. Enough had already happened that he certainly did not trust that the rest of the trip would be uneventful. This was fairly deserted territory; they had met no one on the path that morning. It was a good place for robbers. After all, it had happened once; it could happen again. And if anyone became ill or was hurt they might find themselves out in the bush with night coming on again.

To push those thoughts out of his mind, Inuwa made himself think of Birni. Birni. Where everyone was rich and wore nice clothes and had enough to eat. Where food was plentiful and cheap. Where you could buy absolutely anything in the market. Where there was a school four or five times as big as the one at Turwa. Where all the houses were big with metal roofs instead of grass roofs. And, remembering the brass ring in his ear, where no one could know that he did not really deserve the brass ring and would think he was someone important.

Inuwa called to the others with an exuberance he had not shown before. "Let's go, let's go. On to Birni, the Beautiful City!" It put them in a gay mood as they collected their loads.

The *harmattan* was much heavier now. They could see such a short distance ahead that the path was difficult to follow. In fact, as they started on again Inuwa was not sure they were even on a path. It did not look much like one, but there had been no place to turn off, so this must be it.

They walked and walked. But now there were bushes right in the middle of the path—if it was a path. Finally, as the early dusk was setting in Inuwa said, "This doesn't really look like a path, does it? Do you know the way, Saratu?"

"I have been down this path before but not when the

harmattan was so heavy," Saratu said. "It looks as if we have lost the way."

Inuwa shivered in the chill of the oncoming evening. But it was not only the cold that caused his quivering. They were alone in the bush and night was coming on. Again, he was to be trapped in the bush with darkness on its way!

Chapter 5

A MAD DOG

"We have already spent one night in the bush. I guess we can do it again," said Inuwa's father.

"You mean you have forgotten what happened that night?" asked Inuwa, his hand gripping his sling very hard as he thought of it.

"No, but if we are going to have to stay here we might as well be calm about it," replied his father.

"If only we had Tursinda," said Inuwa softly, "he could warn us of danger."

"I'm cold," said Saratu, shivering. The night chill had found them.

"Listen!" said Inuwa's father.

Everyone was still. There was only the sound of crickets and night birds. Then over to the right they heard the barking of a dog.

"That has to be someone's compound. No dog would be far from home this time of night. Let's go in that direction," said Mallam Yaga.

Without another word the line of three turned to the right. They walked in silence listening for the dog's bark. It came again, and they all stepped up their pace as if at a signal.

They walked quite a distance while no one made a sound that they could help. There was only the pat of soft footsteps on the dusty ground. The sun was behind the thick clouds of dust at the horizon. It would soon cease to give light to the earth, for there was no twilight here.

Inuwa wondered if Saratu was becoming terribly tired. He was very weary himself, and after all, she was a girl. And he was thirsty, but this was no time to stop for a drink. He just wanted to keep going, to hurry out of this terrifying bush into a warm, safe compound.

Again came the dog's bark, much closer. Then through the dust they saw the flicker of fire. Someone's compound fire! Now suddenly their fears were gone. Inuwa laughed in relief.

"Do you suppose we might be in time for food?" said Saratu.

"I could use something to fill up this hole inside of me," said Inuwa.

What a welcome sight they glimpsed through the open compound door. A woman was serving food to two men sitting around a roaring fire in the middle of the compound.

Mallam Yaga called, "*Salaam aleakum*, peace to you."

One man at the fire immediately turned toward the gate and answered, "*Lalay*, welcome." Then he stood up quickly and came to meet them.

He looked at the man and the two children in surprise. "How did you get here?"

"We lost our way and were so glad to hear your dog barking," said Mallam Yaga.

"Yes," laughed the man. "My dog loves to chase cats. He has one up that tree." They all turned to look, even Mallam Yaga turned in that direction. There was the dog, still barking, dancing around the tree in which sat a cat, completely ignoring the nuisance below her.

"Come on in," said the man. "You are indeed lucky to have found our compound. There isn't another for many miles. You are in time for something to eat." He bowed and said, "My name is Mallam Yusufu."

Mallam Yaga introduced himself and the children. Mallam Yusufu led the way to the fire and indicated a seat for Inuwa's father. It was understood that the children would be fed elsewhere, and Inuwa and Saratu stood back, waiting to be told where to go.

From out of the shadows, for it was dark now, came a boy about Inuwa's age. He spoke to the children. "Mother says you should eat with us over here."

Inuwa and Saratu followed the boy. He led them to the grass mat shelter that was part of his mother's cooking house. There was a stool for Inuwa and a stone for Saratu to sit on. Almost immediately they were handed a bowl of guinea corn mush to share. On top of the mush there had

41

been poured a mixture of spinach and dried beans cooked together with spices.

With a quick "Thank you," Inuwa broke off a chunk of the mush and dipped it into some of the spinach mix. Saratu did the same. How good it tasted. The boy of the compound was also eating from a bowl he shared with his mother and another small child. The shelter under which they sat was bright from the light of the cooking fire.

The dog came now and sidled up to the boy, begging for food.

"Yakub, don't feed that dog," commanded his mother.

As soon as she looked away, Yakub slipped a piece of mush to the dog. Inuwa caught the boy's eye and winked.

The boy smiled. "What's your name?" he asked.

"Inuwa, and this is Saratu. We are all going to the hospital at Birni. We got lost from the path and heard your dog bark. Are we near the road here?"

"No, it is way over there," Yakub pointed. "You really did wander off the path, and there are no more compounds for a long way. You were lucky to find ours."

Suddenly Yakub noticed the ring in Inuwa's ear. "How did you win your brass earring?" he asked with interest.

Inuwa looked at his bowl. "By being the best shot with a sling."

"You must be good!" Yakub gave an approving nod.

"He is!" said Saratu, looking at Inuwa with eyes of pride.

Quickly Inuwa said, "Why are you so far from other compounds?"

"My father is a medicine *dokita* and does not want to be near lots of people."

"Who do you play with?" asked Saratu.

"My dog," replied Yakub.

"I had to leave my dog at home. Sure wish I could have brought him."

"It's probably just as well you didn't. Someone came here from Birni today. He said there are rabid dogs between here and there, and in Birni too. You would not want your dog to get close to them."

"No, I sure wouldn't," said Inuwa.

It did not take long to finish the bowl of food. Inuwa had a pleasantly full feeling. He finished off with a big bowl of water that the woman gave him.

42

The woman spoke. "You children probably want to go to bed right away. You must be tired."

Inuwa was tired, but he wanted a chance to pet Yakub's dog. He was glad when Yakub went with him to the house where he was to sleep. The dog was at his heels. The woman took Saratu to another house.

Inuwa sat down on the mat that was to be his. He whistled softly to the dog. The dog came to him, wagging his tail, and lay down with his head in Inuwa's lap.

"That's the first time he's ever done that to a stranger," said Yakub in surprise.

Conversation came easily now. The two boys sat with the dog between them and talked on and on about their dogs.

Then Inuwa ventured, "People must come a long way to see your father."

"Yes, they come many miles. One came today from far on the other side of Birni. He arrived just before you did. He must leave in the morning, so Baba will talk with him tonight."

"Do you ever listen to them?" asked Inuwa.

"I'm not supposed to, but I do once in a while."

Inuwa would not have dared ask just anyone, but he felt he could ask this new friend. "Could we watch, just a little bit?"

Yakub looked doubtful and then said cautiously, "If you will promise not to say a word while we watch and never to tell anyone."

Inuwa nodded eagerly.

Yakub still hesitated. "Promise in Tursinda's name?"

"Promise!"

"All right, come on."

Yakub told his dog to stay at the sleeping house. Not even their footsteps could be heard on the hard earth of the compound as Yakub led the way between the houses, around a pot-bellied mud storage bin, to another house. Then he dropped to his knees and began to crawl. Inuwa did the same. They came to a grass mat shelter that extended out from Mallam Yusufu's house. Voices came from the other side. Yakub sat on his knees and looked through a small hole in the grass mat. He motioned for Inuwa to do the same.

43

Through a hole Inuwa could see two men seated cross-legged on the ground. Beyond them was a fire. Inuwa wished he were closer to the fire; he was cold.

The two men had been talking before the boys came. Now, as they talked, Mallam Yusufu was doing something on the ground between them. First he pushed up a small mound of fine sand, smoothing it very carefully. Then he deftly made a dent in the pile of sand with his finger.

"Before you tell me what your problem is, you may put a coin here," instructed Mallam Yusufu.

The other man instantly produced a coin, which he dropped into the dent in the sand. It looked like a shilling to Inuwa.

Mallam Yusufu sat now without talking, looking at the pile of sand. He slowly drew a ring around the sand with his right forefinger. Then with swift movements of his hand he divided the mound into three equal piles.

"You have a most difficult problem, my friend. It is more complicated by the fact that there are three possible answers to it."

"That's right," said the man in surprise. "But I hadn't told you that yet."

Mallam Yusufu smiled wisely.

After a moment he said, "All right, now you may tell me about your problem."

The man began. "Last rainy season a very expensive blanket was stolen from a compound in our village. In taking the blanket, the person left a footprint in the mud by the door. They were never able to find the man who had made the footprint, but word went out through the village that a curse had been placed on the man, and . . ." The man stopped, swallowed and went on. "And . . . that he would die because of that foot." By the time the man finished he was very upset, trembling.

Mallam Yusufu said quietly, "And you are that man."

"Yes!" the man cried. "Yes! I don't know how you knew, but that's right." He thrust his right foot out in front of him. "Do you see that black spot on my foot? It is getting bigger and bigger. I'm scared, Mallam Yusufu. What shall I do?" His voice had risen higher and higher.

"You may be sure your secret is safe with me. Now let's talk about what you can do. We said there are three things

44

you can do. One, you could go to the man and admit what you did. That might cause the thing on your foot to go away, and then again it may be too late. Two, you could return the blanket and the spot might go away. Three, you could go to the white *dokita* in Birni who has very strong medicine that does not seem to be affected by black men's curses."

"That's right, that's right!" cried the man. "What shall I do?"

"Did you come prepared to pay for my advice?"

"Oh, yes, whatever you say."

"This is very difficult, very difficult, indeed. And, of course, I will need some compensation for keeping your secret. Ordinarily it would cost a big ram and two pounds in cash." Mallam Yusufu was thinking. "But since you are in a hurry, I believe six pounds should cover it all. Did you bring that much?"

The man swallowed hard and said, "Yes, that is exactly what I brought." He reached deep into his robe pocket and brought out a leather wallet from which he took six one-pound notes. These he laid on the mounds of sand between them.

"Thank you," said Mallam Yusufu as he picked them up. "It will be necessary for me to think about this until morning. I will give you my answer then." He stood up.

Yakub gave a pull on Inuwa's arm, and they silently slipped away back to their house.

"Thanks, Yakub," said Inuwa. "But how will I ever know what he tells the man in the morning?"

"You will probably never know," answered Yakub. "And you must never ever mention anything about what you heard."

"Never!" said Inuwa emphatically.

Inuwa dropped to sleep almost as soon as he lay down, so grateful to be here instead of lying fearfully awake out in the bush.

He wakened the next morning with Saratu shaking him gently. His first thought was, "What will Mallam Yusufu tell the man?" He wished Yakub would wake up just in case he might be able to find out the decision.

He turned his attention to getting their things ready for

what should be their last day on the road. As he left the house he intentionally made some noise, but Yakub slept on. The dog followed his every step. Inuwa petted him and talked to him.

Mallam Yusufu's wife served them hot tea and bean cakes. Yakub showed up, sleepy-eyed, as they were saying their thanks. They were on their way before the sun was up. No opportunity presented itself to talk with Yakub.

They made good time. The *harmattan* had vanished in the night, which meant the day would be very hot. But Inuwa could now see that the path was well marked, so he led the way easily, guiding his father. Saratu followed. Mallam Yaga talked, as much to himself as to anyone. Children did not usually converse at length with their fathers, so Inuwa listened and spoke only now and then. He almost wished that Saratu was in front. Even if she was a girl, she was someone to talk with.

At the junction with the road that they should have been on the night before, they paused for a drink and to rest. It was evident that the road going to Birni was well-marked. They would not get lost again.

"We will get to stop at Mallam Birama's compound after all," said Saratu. "I do know where it is now that we are on the main road. It is on up this path a little way." She pointed. "It looks as if we will be in time for morning food."

That sounded good, and they moved quickly to pick up their loads and be on their way.

As Inuwa brushed by Saratu, he slipped one of his pieces of candy to her and said casually, "Why don't you walk up front for a while?"

Saratu said nothing, just nodded and gave a little smile.

As they walked down the wide path, Saratu began to talk, more than Inuwa had heard her do before. She was full of questions. "Does Tursinda do tricks? Did you teach them to him? Where does he sleep? Is he a good watchdog?"

Inuwa answered her questions gladly, enjoying talking about his dog and surprised and pleased that Saratu was interested. She wasn't so bad after all.

The road was easy to travel. The sun was not hot yet. The conversation was pleasant.

Suddenly without warning, a dog came rushing toward

them. He had come out of the bushes along the road. There was unmistakable foam at his mouth, and he was snarling.

"That's a rabid dog!" shouted Inuwa. "Look out!"

Chapter 6

AN UNHAPPY WELCOME

"Run, Saratu! Hide in the bushes!"

Inuwa dropped the guide stick, grabbed the gourd from his head and tossed it aside. The dog was coming too fast to hope to lead his father out of the way. His only chance was to try to do enough damage with his sling to deter the dog until his father could get away.

Saratu started to run, then turned swiftly toward Mallam Yaga. She shouted, "I'll take care of your father!" She snatched the sack of grain from Mallam Yaga's head, setting it down hard on the ground. Then she propelled the blind man by the arm as quickly as possible off the road toward the bushes. Inuwa let fly a stone.

With his father out of the way, Inuwa could run too. But it was too late; the dog was only a few feet away. The animal was no longer running. He had dropped to the ground and was crawling on his belly toward Inuwa. Inuwa raised his sling and aimed again.

But the dog's eyes had a glassy stare, and suddenly he convulsed. He was in the final stages of rabies. Inuwa waited no longer but raced to a small tree and began climbing it. A few feet up he stopped to see if the dog had followed him. He need not have worried. The dog was dead, the convulsion being his last.

Inuwa let himself down the tree slowly. When he reached the ground, he discovered his legs were so weak that he had to lean against the tree.

Saratu came cautiously from her place beside Mallam Yaga and saw the dog no longer moving. She made a wide circle and approached Inuwa. As soon as he saw her, he stood up straight although his legs were still wobbly.

"Weren't you afraid, Inuwa?" said Saratu. "I was."

Inuwa wondered why girls could admit they were scared when boys could not.

"Oh, a little," he said finally.

"It was wonderful the way you stayed there with that dog coming right toward you!" Saratu went on.

Mallam Yaga had made his way back to them. "Inuwa," he said in a husky voice.

"Yes, Baba?"

His father followed the sound of the voice and put his hand on Inuwa's shoulder. "Saratu told me what was happening. I am proud of you, son."

Inuwa was embarrassed. "There wasn't much else to do," he said, shrugging his shoulders. He wanted to change the subject. "Let's go on. It is food time."

"I just lost my appetite," said Mallam Yaga.

"Me too," said Saratu.

Inuwa realized that he too did not find the prospect of food as pleasing as he had a few minutes before.

They went to collect their loads where they had dumped them in their haste. This time Saratu stayed at the end of the line.

Mallam Birama's compound was but a short distance up the road. They were glad to reach it. Food was ready for them soon after they arrived, and by then they had regained their appetites. When they had eaten, they all wanted to relax in the shade.

Inuwa and his father were together. "Inuwa, that mad dog gave us such a scare that I'm going to suggest we rest here a while. Mallam Birama invited us to stay overnight, so I think we will accept his offer."

Inuwa slept much of the afternoon but had no trouble going to sleep that night. He wanted to be fully alert when they reached Birni. If he had to leave Tursinda then he was going to make the most of the journey and see everything there was to see in Birni.

They would start early and hoped to reach Birni after the sun started down the western sky.

Inuwa needed no second call the next morning. Once again they were served food and given some to take with them. The sun was an orange ball as it rose through the dust on the horizon. *Harmattan* was not heavy but enough to keep the day a bit cool.

There was an air of gaiety about the three as they trotted along the path. Inuwa sang some songs he had learned in school. Saratu knew some of them too and joined in. When they stopped singing, Mallam Yaga would call for more.

They halted their singing as they neared Birni. There were more and more people in the road. No one greeted them. That was unusual. At Turwa everyone gave a greeting even if they did not know each other.

So many compounds! Birni was indeed a big town. The hospital was in the heart of the town. Inuwa asked directions and they moved down the main street.

Inuwa could not seem to look fast enough to see everything. So many bicycles. A big lorry rattled down the street. There were men seated by little tables along the road selling soap, matches, cigarettes and candy. Inuwa was amazed. Did people buy candy just any time?

And there was a woman cooking bean cakes right there beside the road. A person could buy them hot right from the cooking oil. The smell was tantalizing. So many houses had tin roofs, which shone in the sun. There was only one such roof in Turwa. That belonged to the school teacher. But here many buildings had tin roofs.

They passed five different shops where cloth, shirts, food and *Krola* were sold. Turwa had only one tiny shop. What a wonderful place Birni was! Even better than he had imagined.

For a few brief moments he forgot who he was and what he was doing. He stood staring at some children playing with a ball, only it was very light and would sail away if they did not have it tied to a string in their hand. He started on without looking ahead first.

Suddenly there was a mad ringing of a bicycle bell and the angry shouts of its rider. "Watch where you are going, you dirty *banza* Munga boy!"

Inuwa looked around, wondering to whom the man would say such a terrible thing. A dirty no-good boy from the Munga tribe, the man had said. But Inuwa saw no other boy with an earring in his ear. Then a sick feeling came into his stomach. The man had been talking about him!

50

*Men sat at little tables selling soap, matches,
cigarettes and candy.*

Chapter 7

THE HOSPITAL AT LAST

"Baba! Why did he say that?" cried Inuwa.

His father answered softly. "Most of the people of this village are of the Waya tribe. People had told me that they hated other tribes. They feel that the hospital belongs only to them."

"But will they treat us like that in the hospital?"

"No, they say that everyone receives equal treatment there. But not so in the village."

Inuwa was sorry they had come. Didn't these people know that his village had more children in school than any for ten miles in all directions? They should know that a boy from Turwa had won the first prize in a farm show for the best head of guinea corn in all the province, including Birni.

They started on. Inuwa was hurt and angry, but this time he watched where he was going. Soon they saw the long low buildings of the hospital.

"Baba! Here we are! At last! The place to make you see again!"

Mallam Yaga stopped and stood staring with sightless eyes. "If only it is possible," he said softly.

They asked directions to the dispensary building and found it without difficulty. The man in charge was just closing the window, but he explained what they should do. Mallam Yaga would be seen first by the male nurse, Mallam Yohanna, who was in charge of the dispensary. Then if Mallam Yohanna thought he needed to be seen by the doctor, he would refer him on to the doctor. But first Mallam Yaga could be registered, which would save time the next morning.

"Inuwa, we might as well have Mallam Yohanna see you too while we are here," said his father.

The man directed them to the office where they could register.

"I hope I don't have to have injections," said Saratu.

"Oh, but shots are the very best medicine you can get," declared Inuwa.

"I don't think I want the best medicine then. I'm not brave like you are," returned Saratu.

Inuwa's pride was momentarily restored, and he stood very straight as they waited in line to register. They each received a number written on a card. They were to bring that number with them each time they came to the hospital. If it was lost it would cost a toro to get a new one. Inuwa hid his card carefully deep in the pocket of his shorts. A toro would buy six pieces of candy.

After that they were told that they were to give a specimen to the laboratory, so they did that. That was all they could do that day, so they asked where they could stay for the night. A man led them to a small round house on the hospital grounds. It was one of many just like it. People were everywhere, people who, like themselves, were at the hospital for treatment.

Saratu set about arranging their belongings. They would all sleep in the small house. She would cook outside over an open fire.

"Let's see if you can keep the guinea corn mush from being lumpy," teased Inuwa.

Saratu looked at him in her shy way and said, "I'll try."

Inuwa knew it would take a while to prepare supper, so he went off to explore the hospital. The next day he would have to search for wood. It could be bought here, but it was terribly expensive. In fact, if he worked hard he could collect enough wood for their own needs and to sell too.

There were perhaps fifteen of the mud houses with grass roofs like the one they were staying in. There was not another empty one. Apparently they were lucky to get that one. There was a long building with perhaps ten rooms in it in which people were staying. Also grass-mat shelters had been put up. There must have been several hundred people altogether living on the hospital grounds. What were all of them doing there, Inuwa wondered.

It was evening and in front of every house or shelter a woman or a girl cooked over an open fire. Most of them were preparing guinea corn mush, a few were boiling rice. Inuwa walked down the rows of houses with the wonderful smells coming from the cooking pots. Here someone had fish *panya*; there was tomato and chunks of meat boiling together with spices. There was a quiet hum of voices. Small children played beside their mothers or cooed on their mothers' backs. It made Inuwa a little homesick.

He stopped suddenly and stared. Three young boys were standing near what looked like a stick coming out of the ground. One of the boys would push on the stick and water would come out. When he took his hand away, it stopped. Inuwa moved closer to see this strange gadget. He would like a drink if he could make the thing work. Maybe the boys would show him how.

He walked up to them and said, "Hello," in English.

The three boys looked at him but said nothing. Then they all moved away still without speaking. Inuwa wondered what was wrong. Did his clothes look funny? He glanced down at his shirt and shorts. They were no different than those of the three boys. Then he remembered ... the earring in his ear that marked him as a Munga. But what was wrong with being a Munga?

He pushed on the stick that came out of the ground as he had seen the boys do it. Water came gushing out. He took a drink and walked on.

He turned toward one of the hospital buildings. It looked as if most of the patients were outside on the verandah that ran all the way around the building. There were children on their mothers' backs or being held, some asleep, some crying, some nursing. There were bandaged arms, legs, heads. What a lot of sick children!

"*Wana*," someone said. Inuwa turned sharply, suspiciously. Who would be speaking to him in the Munga language? There, sitting on the verandah with his feet dangling over the edge, was a boy with a wire earring in one ear. He was wearing khaki-colored shorts and a ragged tee shirt.

"*Wana*," returned Inuwa eagerly. "Am I glad to see you!"

"Same here. I'm Bitrus from the village of Nasa."

"My village is Turwa. I'm Inuwa Gwonza."

"Have you been having trouble too?" asked Bitrus.

Inuwa nodded. "Why don't they like us?"

Bitrus shrugged his shoulders. "Wish I knew. I have learned to pay no attention, but sometimes it makes me mad."

Bitrus moved his head so that he could see Inuwa's left ear better. "A brass ring! Hey, that's all right. How did you do it?"

Inuwa looked down. "I'm pretty good with a slingshot."

"Pretty good! You can't be just pretty good and earn a brass ring. You must have . . ."

Inuwa interrupted, pointing to the bandage on Bitrus' leg. "Did you hurt yourself?"

"It is an ulcer. I've been here two months. The doctor says I may go home next week. My leg is about healed. They had to take some skin off my thigh and put it on the sore to make it close up."

"*Aiya*, did it hurt?"

The boy nodded. "They put me to sleep to take off the skin, but it hurt where they took it off. It is healed now." He showed the scar on his thigh. A shiver went through Inuwa. Would they do that to Saratu?

"I'm looking the hospital over. We just arrived this afternoon," said Inuwa.

"Fine. Let me show you around. There isn't a spot that I don't know by heart. Come on."

"Are you allowed to leave the children's building?" asked Inuwa in surprise.

Bitrus laughed. "I go anywhere I want to."

Bitrus led the way, limping slightly. "This first building is the surgery where they operate on people."

Just then out of one of the doors came a white man, taking long strides.

"*Wana, dokita*," said Bitrus with a bow as the man reached them. Quickly Inuwa bowed too and murmured, "*Wana*."

"Hello, there, Bitrus," said the doctor in English. "How are you today?"

"Very well, thank you," answered Bitrus in English.

And the doctor hurried down the sidewalk.

"Is that the *dokita*? Why, he's really friendly," said Inuwa in surprise.

"He is a nice fellow. I like him," replied Bitrus.

"I just supposed you never saw the *dokita* except when you were very sick."

"Oh, no. He will stop and talk if he has time, but if he doesn't he at least greets you. He is terribly busy with so many people coming to the hospital now in dry season."

"Does he always talk in English?" asked Inuwa.

"No. He knows the Diya language very well and some Munga. But he knows that I want to learn English, so he helps me."

"My father is blind. We hope the *dokita* can make him see."

"I've really learned a lot since I came here. I found out that there are several things that can cause blindness. If it is something the *dokita* can operate on he uses the tiniest tool you ever saw and cuts into the eye to take out the blind part."

"And if he can't operate?"

"Sometimes he gives medicine. Sometimes there is nothing he can do if it is too far along. Did you know that those tiny flies that bite you when you are out in the bush along rivers can make you blind?"

"If only he can help my father. If he could just see again!"

Around the corner of the surgery building came a white-uniformed worker pulling a table with wheels. On it was a woman with a sheet over her. The *dokita* was behind pushing the table. The boys stepped back out of the way. Bitrus whispered as they went past. "That woman has been in labor since day before yesterday. They just brought her to the hospital this morning. Now they are going to have to cut open her stomach and take the baby out."

"But the baby will be dead?" ventured Inuwa.

"Maybe, maybe not. A lot of them are still alive."

"I wish I could watch," said Inuwa.

"No one gets to watch except the hospital workers."

Down the verandah came a man dressed all in white. An insignia on his shirt said, "Registered Nurse."

"Who is that?" asked Inuwa.

"That is Mallam James. He is one of the nurses. His job is to be in charge of one of the wards. That's what they call the various houses. Today he is to help in surgery too," replied Bitrus.

56

"You sure know a lot about what goes on around here."

"So will you when you have been here two months."

"I wouldn't want to stay two months. I've got a dog . . ."

Bitrus did not let him finish. He said eagerly, "So have I. She was supposed to have pups soon after I left. I can hardly wait to see them. They will be big enough to wean."

A truck drove into the hospital grounds.

"Hey, come on, let's see what the native authority truck from Kabuk has brought. They don't have a hospital there, so the government truck has to bring serious patients here." He said this as he was walking rapidly toward the truck. Inuwa followed closely.

As soon as the truck stopped, two men climbed out. From the bed of the truck a man was already handing down sacks and gourds full of things to people standing near. Moans came from the back of the truck. Someone had gone to bring the stretcher. A nurse, Mallam Lifa, was summoned, and he gave instructions for moving the person.

As the men were lifting the patient to the stretcher, the boys could see that it was a woman. One of her legs was broken with the bone sticking through the skin. The wound was ugly and smelled terrible. Bitrus, with no hesitancy, walked over beside the driver of the truck and asked questions. He returned to Inuwa and explained.

"That man's wife fell out of a tree when she was cutting branches for wood. That was yesterday morning. They live miles from Kabuk. Looks like the *dokita* will have another emergency operation to do today. It is a rare day that he doesn't have at least one emergency." Bitrus spoke the words, emergency operation, in English, slowly and with pride.

The boys watched as the woman was carried to the surgery building. Then Bitrus led the way toward some other buildings.

"These two are men's and women's wards."

"Have there been many patients coming with *mindi*?" asked Inuwa.

"Yes. That building way off from the others is for *mindi* patients." Bitrus pointed. "There is medicine here for it if people come in time."

They walked on a little way. "That building is where

57

women have their babies. The little one beside it is where they store all the medicines and supplies. Then that one over there by the road is the one where you will take your father to see the *dokita*, and the one beside it is the place to get injections and medicine."

"Saratu doesn't want to take shots," said Inuwa.

"Who is Saratu?"

Inuwa shrugged his shoulders. "Oh, she is just the girl who came along from Ghong. She does our cooking. Who cooks your food?"

"My mother is here. We sure will be glad to start for home. Two months is a long time. We ran out of food and had to send word for someone to bring more. Which reminds me, I'm hungry. Let's go eat."

Inuwa's stomach agreed. He walked back with Bitrus to the little room in one of the long buildings in which Bitrus' mother stayed. He greeted her and then threaded his way between the cooking fires back to his house.

Saratu saw him coming. "Where have you been? The food is ready."

"I found a boy from Nasa. He showed me around the hospital." Inuwa sat down and waited for Saratu to bring his food. His father was already eating, seated nearby.

The food tasted good; Saratu had done a good job, but he had to tease her. He frowned and growled, "I found some lumps in my mush."

Suddenly Saratu was in tears. She left the food she was eating and went running out of sight. Inuwa could have kicked himself. Now she would never believe he was teasing. He did know she would not return to eat while he was there, so he finished and went off to find Bitrus.

He and Bitrus were listening to the evening religious song service when Inuwa suddenly had an idea. He would give his last piece of candy to Saratu to show he was sorry.

"I just remembered something," he whispered to Bitrus and slipped away. When he reached the house, he found Saratu asleep on her mat. Now what should he do?

Chapter 8

THE THIEF

As soon as he awakened the next morning, Inuwa sat up. He saw that Saratu and his father were already out of the house. Mallam Yaga would want to get to the dispensary early.

He stepped outside and called to Saratu. "We want to be first in line to see Mallam Yohanna. Is there something we could eat right away?"

She did not look at him, only nodded.

Inuwa noted with surprise that his father was already eating. "Saratu must have gotten up in the dark to have food ready already."

Mallam Yaga nodded. "It is very good too."

As she served him a bowl of thin hot mush, Inuwa reached into his pocket for the candy, but before he could give it to her . . .

"*Wana*," called Bitrus as he approached them.

"*Wana*, Bitrus," said Inuwa with forced enthusiasm.

"*Wana*, Saratu," he addressed her. She looked up in surprise that he knew her name, then, embarrassed, looked down again.

"Baba and I will be first in line to see Mallam Yohanna," stated Inuwa.

"That's good." He turned again to Saratu. "You will probably have to see the doctor too about your leg. But there is plenty of time. I'll take you on a quick tour of the hospital if you would like."

Saratu looked at him with a shy smile and nodded.

Inuwa frowned to himself but said nothing. He did not feel so good about Bitrus' being with Saratu.

Inuwa led his father to the verandah of the dispensary building, gave the doorkeeper their cards and sat down to wait. There were five people ahead of them.

People began coming and soon they were sitting or standing everywhere. Sick babies were whining and crying. People talked with each other in low voices, telling of where they had come from and about the illnesses that had brought them to Birni. Inuwa heard many languages being spoken. He tried to count but lost track at seventy-five. He was glad they had arrived early and wondered about Saratu.

Just as the doorkeeper called for them, Inuwa saw Saratu making her way through the crowd.

He guided Mallam Yaga through the door and to a place on a bench inside. His father was very nervous.

"This is it, Inuwa. Now we find out if I will ever see again. May God go with us."

As they waited their turn again, Inuwa watched Mallam Yohanna with great interest. People came and sat on a stool in front of the nurse. First he talked to them, asked them questions. Then he put two things into his ears and laid the other end on the patient's chest and back. One was a baby, and he also used a thing that he held up to the baby's ears. Then he put a flat stick on the baby's tongue and looked into its mouth. That made the baby cry.

After he had talked with and examined a patient, he would write something down on a card and motion for the person to go sit down on another bench. Soon that person would be called by one of the other hospital workers sitting at the table who would give them cards. Inuwa found later that they had to have these in order to get their daily medicine or injections. They paid their money and went out the far door.

By this time there were many people in the room. It was very noisy with two babies crying and small children fussing. The workers were trying to talk above the noise and having to repeat to be heard. There was the sound of money clinking as people paid their bills.

Then it was Mallam Yaga's turn. Inuwa led him to the stool in front of Mallam Yohanna. He stayed near as his father explained how the blindness came about. The nurse listened closely, nodding now and then, asking questions. When Mallam Yaga finished, the nurse felt his skin and looked at his feet and legs. He asked more questions.

Then he took a little shiny stick that had a light on one end and looked closely at Mallam Yaga's eyes, taking a long time to do it. "You say you can see only light and darkness in both eyes?" Mallam Yaga nodded. The nurse pondered. He picked up the instrument with the light on the end and once again looked carefully at both his eyes.

"I am going to send you to see the *dokita*." He motioned to the attendant. "Go with the mañ to the *dokita*'s office. Here is his record." He handed some papers to the attendant.

The nurse glanced down at the next card. "Oh, you want to be examined too?" he asked of Inuwa.

Inuwa nodded, suddenly wishing he could say no.

The attendant led Mallam Yaga to another chair, and Inuwa sat down in front of Mallam Yohanna.

The nurse looked at the card in front of him on which had been recorded the results of the laboratory work done the day before. He looked up at Inuwa and said, "Well, young man, do you like injections?"

Inuwa gulped and was not sure what to say.

"Your laboratory report shows that you have schistosomiasis, which will require twelve shots. They are given three times a week, which means you will need to stay here a month. Can you do that?"

If his father had to stay he might as well get the injections. He turned to Mallam Yaga who nodded.

"The cost is seventeen shillings, which must be paid before they start the injections. The first one will be tomorrow morning."

The nurse examined Inuwa, looking at his eyes, ears and into his mouth. He felt deep into Inuwa's stomach until it hurt. Mallam Yohanna frowned. "You'd better get those injections; your liver and spleen are enlarged."

Then he smiled at Inuwa and said, "That's all."

Inuwa counted out seventeen shillings from the bag of coins his father gave him and watched the clerk mark "Paid" on his record.

Then he and his father followed the attendant across the yard to the surgery building and at his direction sat down on the cool verandah. The day was going to be hot; they should enjoy the coolness while they could.

Almost immediately a young girl in a white uniform came out and said, "The *dokita* can see you now."

Inuwa noticed that a name tag on her pocket said, "Mallama Maryamu." She was a nurse too.

The *dokita* did just what Mallam Yohanna had done, asking questions, looking into Mallam Yaga's eyes with the tiny light. The way the *dokita* spoke was strange, even though it was in the Munga language. When Mallam Yaga did not seem to understand, Mallama Maryamu would repeat it.

Finally the *dokita* leaned back in his chair and said, "The only chance you have is an operation. I would take out the part of the eye that is cloudy, which is not letting the light in. Then if the rest of your eye is all right you should be able to see again. But we wouldn't know that for sure until five days after the operation."

The *dokita* waited for Maryamu to repeat it.

"You mean . . . you mean I may be able to see again?" asked Mallam Yaga breathlessly.

"Yes," replied the *dokita*. "Not as well as you did before, but good enough to hoe your farm and do everything for yourself. The operation will cost two pounds. I would want you to take medicine for two weeks to build up your strength. We could do the surgery two weeks from next market day. Can you wait until then?"

"Yes, I'll wait," said Mallam Yaga quickly.

Inuwa broke in. "Will my father really see again?"

"I can't promise, but we will do what we can."

"We will be so thankful!" said Inuwa.

The *dokita* stood up. "I see you are from Turwa. A man from that village had this operation. Let's see . . . Maryamu, do you remember his name?"

Inuwa interrupted. "It was Mallam Zakama. That is why my father decided to come. Mallam Zakama is getting along very well now."

The *dokita* went on gravely, "They are not all that fortunate. Mallama Maryamu will give you the necessary cards for medicine to take until time for the operation."

Inuwa took his father to the line to await the pills while he went back into the dispensary to pay for them. When he returned, the line had moved only a little. He was impatient to be on his way after wood before it got any hotter.

Finally, Mallam Yaga was through and Inuwa led him back to the house. Bitrus had told him where to go after wood. It was a long way, and the sun was already hot on his shoulders.

After getting a drink at the water pipe, he started off at a trot. His stomach said it was empty. Normally they would eat about this time, but the early morning mush was all they would have until evening. The smell of food from many cooking pots made his mouth water.

Then he came upon one of the delights of Birni, a woman cooking peanut sticks right beside the road. A fat clay pot sat on stones over a small fire. Out of the bubbling oil she lifted brown crunchy peanut sticks.

Inuwa felt his pocket. Yes, the *kobo,* a one-cent piece, which he had dropped into his pocket yesterday was there. It was enough for three peanut sticks.

Off he went down the path, thinking again how great a place Birni was.

When he returned with a load of wood on his head, it was late afternoon. He dropped the heavy load behind the house and walked around to the front. Saratu was there. To his surprise she greeted him. She was different somehow, not shy anymore.

"What did the *dokita* say about your father?" she asked.

"There is a very good chance that he may see again!"

"Really, Inuwa? That's wonderful news!"

"And I have to have injections," Inuwa said with a frown. "How about you?"

"I do too," she said gaily. "I even got my first one today."

"I thought you didn't want shots," said Inuwa almost angrily.

"Oh, I guess they won't be so bad."

Inuwa remembered the scar on Bitrus' leg. "But the ulcer ... what about the ulcer on your leg?"

"I also have to go each day and soak my leg in a bucket of purple-colored water." She laughed. "I'll have a purple leg for a while."

"Then ... then it's not too serious?" asked Inuwa.

"Well . . ." she paused, "the *dokita* sure frowned when he looked at it. Then he said he was glad I had not waited any longer, that the soaking each day should make it heal, but that I must not skip even one day."

Inuwa was not in a very good mood. He really was not looking forward to twelve injections, and now Saratu was suddenly a changed person. He had a sneaking suspicion that Bitrus had something to do with it.

He turned and walked away, going around the little house. Maybe he should put the wood inside the house.

As he came around the house he saw someone picking up some of his sticks.

"Hey!" he yelled. "Leave that alone. That's ours!"

"Is that right, *banza* Munga boy?" the big boy taunted. "What are you going to do about it?" The single braid down his back that marked him as a member of the Diya tribe swung defiantly.

Inuwa was angry, angrier than he had ever been in his life. The boy was much bigger than he, but in three swift leaps Inuwa was in front of him. He gathered all the strength he had and hit the boy squarely on the jaw. The blow knocked the boy down but not out. He bounced back up and grabbed Inuwa, holding him in a tight squeeze. Inuwa could not breathe. He squirmed and wriggled. Things were going black. Then he kicked with all he had. His heel bone landed hard on the boy's shin. The boy gasped with pain and released his hold just enough for Inuwa to turn in his grasp. Inuwa brought up his knee hard in the boy's stomach. The boy silently collapsed, the wind knocked out of him.

Chapter 9

A FAMILIAR STRANGER

Inuwa stood over the boy, angry, glaring. The boy slowly got to his feet, dazed, and stumbled off. A short distance away he stopped and turned.

"You'll be sorry for that, Munga boy," he said.

"Next time you leave my wood alone!" warned Inuwa.

Inuwa's father had been inside the house and now came out, feeling his way along the wall. "What happened, Inuwa?"

"A boy was trying to steal our wood!"

"Why didn't you call me? He would have left when a man came on the scene."

"Yes, but he was stealing our wood!" protested Inuwa. "And he wore his hair braided down the back. The Diya tribe isn't any better than the Munga."

"Of course not. But he obviously doesn't think so. You two boys seem about the same age. Too bad you can't play together instead of fight."

"Be reasonable! Didn't you hear me say he was stealing the wood I walked miles to get?"

"Yes, but several people have warned us not to leave anything where it would be a temptation. Better bring the wood around near the door."

"Oh, all right," muttered Inuwa. What was he supposed to do, let that Diya boy take his wood? But before he moved the wood, he wandered stealthily around until he spied the Diya boy going into the grass-mat lean-to where he was apparently staying.

Inuwa ate his evening meal in silence, not really aware of what he was eating. Soon after that he lay down on his grass mat. He thought a long time about what his father had said. His final conclusion before dropping off to sleep was that he would do exactly the same thing again.

The next morning Inuwa discovered why a large portion of the people were at the hospital. He was far back in the line waiting for injections. He had time to think about that shot he was going to get. To pass the time he counted the men and boys in line. 197! The women and girls came every other day when the men did not.

By the time he finally reached the man who gave the injections, he was feeling a little sick at his stomach. He clenched his teeth as he bared his right hip. It was over so quickly that he turned around to see if that was all. It had not even hurt.

"Say, that didn't hurt. How come?"

"We keep the needles sharp," replied the man smiling.

Inuwa went out of the injection room in better spirits. This would not be so bad after all. As he pushed the screen door open, he suddenly stopped and shut it again. The boy who had tried to steal his wood was passing the door. When he was safely out of sight, Inuwa went out. This was not going to be much fun if he had to avoid that boy for the rest of the time.

Inuwa went around the corner of the building to watch where the boy was going. He was carrying a dish in his hands and entered the door of the women's ward. Apparently someone in his family was in the women's ward.

The days went by more quickly than Inuwa had thought they would. One morning Saratu would have her injection; the next morning was his turn. Saratu was always among the first to soak her leg.

The doctor had ordered some drinking medicine and pills also for Inuwa's father. So each morning Inuwa would lead his father to the end of the medicine line and leave him while he took his father's other card and went after the pills in another line. On the mornings that he had to stand in line for his injection, Saratu had the food ready long before he got there. Mallam Yaga visited with other men from other villages as he sat under the trees.

Some days Inuwa arose early and went after wood. On other days, he and Bitrus explored the town. (They learned what each canteen sold—fascinating items such as toothbrushes and plastic water bottles.)

On Sunday they all attended the services at the Christian

church. Bitrus went too. The church building was much larger than theirs in Turwa. People wore much nicer clothes. Inuwa looked down at his only pair of shorts and his shirt. He had not noticed that they were dirty; nor had he been aware of the frayed edges on the shorts. Now his shirt had almost more holes than cloth. Maybe he should wash his things tomorrow. He recognized some of the songs that were sung, but the sermon was in the Diya language. After awhile the mud benches became very uncomfortable. He started to whisper to Bitrus, but his father's frown stopped that.

As they left the church and walked down the path toward the hospital no one spoke to them. Many people stared. As they passed a group of children, a stone came flying their way, accompanied by a cry of "*Banza!*" Inuwa took a step toward the group, angry and ready to pull their ears.

Somehow his father was aware of his movement. "Inuwa!" his father called sharply. "Don't stoop to doing something just as bad as what they are doing."

They walked on, with Inuwa seething. One of the small boys ran up close to Inuwa and spat out, "Coward!" Inuwa reached out to grab him. He quickly glanced at his father. Mallam Yaga moved with slow but proud steps, head up. Inuwa turned back to the path and walked on, carefully ignoring the children.

On market day Inuwa and Saratu were up early. Food was eaten quickly. Bitrus and Inuwa were going to market together and Saratu had found a friend to go with. It was Saratu's day for an injection, so the boys left before she did.

The Birni market was just as wonderful as Inuwa thought it would be. There was stall after stall of interesting things. Bitrus enjoyed showing him all the new foods and toys.

There was one place that sold only bicycle parts. Another sold only candy and biscuits. Inuwa had never dreamed there were so many different kinds of candy and biscuits. Material already cut into *zhebi* lengths was displayed in several stalls in a row. There were booths that had only ready-made clothing, shorts and shirts and dresses. There were stalls for leatherwork, brasswork, woven baskets. People had brought peanuts to sell. Pile after pile of peanuts were awaiting a lorry to carry them away.

Finally the boys came to the row upon row of women sitting beside their gourds and baskets full of good things to eat. The women were dressed in brightly colored wrap-around cloths. The baskets held peanut sticks and bean cakes, potato cakes and bread rolls. Fruits of all kinds were in piles on the ground in front of the women. Mangoes, guavas, bananas, grapefruit, oranges, limes. The smell was overwhelming, making Inuwa's stomach cry out.

Inuwa had decided before he came to buy some fruit. At Turwa they rarely had fruit. But what a choice! Unable to decide, he momentarily looked away. His eye caught sight of a big mound of red tomatoes. That was what he wanted. He put down the shilling his grandmother had given him and raised one finger. The woman gave him a big red toma-to and one coin in change. He shook his head and started to hand back the tomato. The woman laid down another coin. He smiled and took it.

The tomato was beautiful. He put it to his lips to take a bite when he thought of his father. Putting down one of the coins, he took another tomato and put it carefully into his pocket. Then he proceeded to eat his own.

The two boys looked at everything there was to eat. A most interesting place was the little covered stall that had beads, earrings and all kinds of trinkets. While Bitrus was looking at something else, Inuwa quickly bought a small round mirror with his last coin. He would give it to Saratu.

"Birni is a grand place," declared Inuwa as they walked back to the hospital.

"Yes, except for . . ." Bitrus did not finish.

"Yes, I know," said Inuwa.

When they reached the hospital Saratu was at their house. "Inuwa, I just discovered that the meat and toma-toes that I bought in market are gone. I made a special trip home with them and then returned to market."

"Wasn't my father here while we were gone? We never leave without someone's being here."

"He says he was sitting over there under that tree but wouldn't have seen it, and if whoever did it was quiet he wouldn't have heard them."

"I'll bet I can guess who did it," said Inuwa, clenching his teeth.

"Well, it makes me mad," declared Saratu. "We barely had enough money to pay for the medicines. Having meat today was to be a special treat."

"That's too bad," said Bitrus.

"Well, we just have to have leaf *panya*," said Saratu "Inuwa, I need some water to wash the leaves in. Would you get some please?"

"Sure." He picked up the gourd they used for carrying water. "Come on, Bitrus, go with me."

"No, I'm tired. I'll wait for you here."

Inuwa eyed him suspiciously but went on.

When he returned he and Bitrus went off to look at the new building going up behind the surgery. As they came around the dispensary building they saw the boy whom Inuwa had hit. He was coming down the path toward them. When he saw them, he suddenly veered off toward the children's ward. "Well," Inuwa thought, "that boy isn't eager to see me either." That would make things easier, but it left Inuwa uneasy.

Inuwa returned to the house when he thought the food would be ready. His bare feet made no noise as he approached, so Saratu did not hear him. She was sitting beside the fire stirring the guinea corn mush. As she stirred, she looked at herself in a small mirror. It looked like the one Inuwa had bought, only he had not given it to her.

"Where did you get that," he asked.

Saratu jumped in surprise and dropped the mirror into her pocket. She said nothing.

"I asked you where you got that. Did you buy it in the market?"

Saratu went back to stirring the mush. She did not look at him as she said, in a tiny voice, "Bitrus gave it to me."

When could Bitrus have bought a mirror when he was with him all the time? And then he beat Inuwa to giving it to Saratu. Inuwa's spirits fell again.

The next day Bitrus and Inuwa were sitting in the shade of the trees near the entrance to the hospital. Interesting things happened there, and they hoped for something exciting today. They were talking about dogs and swimming and fishing when suddenly Bitrus looked up.

"Look! They are bringing someone in on a stretcher."

The boys moved over to the edge of the road and waited for the procession to pass. First came four men, each with a corner of the homemade stretcher on one shoulder. A group of people followed, apparently friends and family of the sick person.

The men set down the stretcher in the shade.

"I'll call Mallam James," offered Bitrus. At a nod from one of the men, he sped off to find the nurse.

He returned quickly with Mallam James following.

Inuwa moved where he could get a better look. The patient's foot was bandaged. Spread over the person on the stretcher was a very pretty blanket, obviously an expensive one. Then Inuwa saw the man's face and gasped. It was the man he and Yakub had watched at Mallam Yusufu's compound!

Chapter 10

AN ENEMY IN NEED

Inuwa edged a little closer. Was he sure? Yes, there was no doubt about it. This was the same man who had come to Mallam Yusufu for advice. Was this what Mallam Yusufu had told him? But that was over two weeks ago. Why was the man here now?

Bitrus saw Inuwa's puzzled look. "What's the matter?" he asked.

"Do you think you could find out what is wrong with this man? Could you ask Mallam James?"

"Sure. We will have to wait until the *dokita* sees him though."

The *dokita* came very soon to examine the patient. He asked the people to move back. Inuwa and Bitrus stepped back but they watched closely.

The dokita pulled up the blanket and then unwrapped a dirty cloth from the man's foot. When he saw the foot, Inuwa gasped again. The black place was several times bigger than when he had seen it only two weeks before. Now it covered most of the foot in front of the ankle. What could it be to grow like that?"

The *dokita* examined the man carefully, feeling under his arms and pushing his hand into his stomach. Finally he rose, said something quietly to Mallam James and returned to his work in the dispensary.

Mallam James called the man who was obviously looking after the sick man.

"Go listen!" whispered Inuwa.

Bitrus scooted quickly behind the tree near where the nurse was talking to the man. Soon the nurse walked away, and the man came back to the stretcher.

Inuwa waited eagerly for Bitrus to return. When he did,

they moved away from the group. "What did he say?" asked Inuwa. "What did he say?"

"He said there was no doubt about it; the man has black melanoma, a fast-growing cancer. The *dokita* said they should take him home because he couldn't possibly last more than a couple weeks."

Inuwa stared at Bitrus, speechless, his eyes wide.

"What's the matter? Do you know the man?" asked Bitrus.

Inuwa remembered the "Never" that he had said in promise to Yakub. "No . . . no . . . I don't know the man."

The day Inuwa's father went into the hospital to await surgery was also the day Bitrus was to leave. Inuwa was silent as he ate his morning food. Mallam Yaga was in good spirits.

"Tomorrow's the day! Then in just five days we will know," said Mallam Yaga.

"Are you a little afraid of the operation, Mallam Yaga?" asked Saratu.

Inuwa stared at Saratu in amazement. Who could ask his father such a question?

Mallam Yaga was silent; finally he said, "Yes, I am afraid."

Inuwa stopped with a piece of mush half way to his mouth. Had he heard right?

His father went on. "But there are times when one must take a chance. I have talked with many people these past weeks and I've heard only praise for this *dokita*."

Inuwa went on eating slowly, his mind on what his father had just said.

When Mallam Yaga was ready, Inuwa guided him up to the men's ward and stayed to see that he was settled in. It would be fun to visit his father in the evenings because there were electric lights in the wards. There was only firelight and a flashlight at their little house.

He told his father he would be back later and went to find Bitrus. Bitrus and his mother were almost ready to leave. Inuwa helped put the load on Bitrus' head and another on his mother's head.

"I almost hate to leave," said Bitrus. "It's been fun here, at least since you came, Inuwa."

"Well, I'm ready to go home!" said his mother emphatically as she started out toward the road. Bitrus and Inuwa followed. As they passed the little round house, Bitrus called good-bye to Saratu. She came running to them and reached up to put something into the gourd Bitrus was carrying.

"That's for you," she said softly.

"Thanks, Saratu. Someday I will get to Ghong and come to greet you."

Inuwa wished he knew what she had given Bitrus. She had never given him anything.

Inuwa walked down the road almost a mile with Bitrus and his mother. Finally he told them good-bye. When he turned back, he ran, not wanting to watch them go.

Mallam Yaga's surgery was scheduled as the first case the next morning. Inuwa was there when they put his father on a stretcher and wheeled him to the surgery building. Inuwa managed to pat his father's hand just as they took him in through the door. Then he sat down on the verandah to wait.

Five days and they would know whether or not his father could see. If only he could! Just think how proud they would all be if Mallam Yaga could walk into their compound without help from anyone. These would be five long days.

When Inuwa thought he just could not wait any longer, the hospital attendants came out pushing the surgery cart. He followed as they made their way up the cement walk to the men's ward. Inuwa ran beside the cart.

"Baba," Inuwa spoke to the bandage-wrapped face.

His father said, "Yes?"

"How do you feel?"

"Fine. The *dokita* said it went well."

Inuwa's heart skipped. Five days! And then?

Inuwa stayed with his father until midafternoon.

When he returned to the house, Saratu was waiting for him. "Someone stole one of our sacks of guinea corn!"

"Oh, no! How could they? Weren't you here all the time?"

"I was gone only a few minutes to bring water."

73

"Do you suppose it was the same boy?" Inuwa set his jaw at the thought.

"I don't know," said Saratu angrily. "It was a good thing I was using some out of each sack, so he got away with only part of a sack."

"Saratu!" Inuwa cried. "The *dokita* said Baba's operation went well!"

"Good, good, good!" Saratu jumped up and down.

"Oh, if only Baba can see again. Just think!"

"Just think!" echoed Saratu.

"In five days they take off the bandages. Then I have one more shot after that. Then we go home! Home, Saratu, home! To see Tursinda!"

Saratu laughed, "That must be a pretty wonderful dog. I'd like to see him."

"I'll bring him to see you," promised Inuwa.

"A whole day's walk just to show me Tursinda? You do like that dog!"

"I . . . like you too, Saratu."

She was embarrassed. Thrusting a bowl toward him, she said, "Here, eat your food."

It was the night of the third day after Mallam Yaga's operation. Inuwa and his father were sitting on benches outside the men's ward. The benches were shared by people from the women's ward too. There was quiet conversation in the cool evening. It was difficult to see people's faces clearly in the dim light from the small bulbs over the doors of the two wards or the yard light some distance away.

"I'm tired, Inuwa. I believe I'll go to bed," said his father.

Inuwa guided his father back into the men's ward and helped him into bed. Then he returned again to the bench. It was so pleasant to sit there. On the bench behind him sat two people whom Inuwa could not see. He could only hear what they were saying.

"The *dokita* says Mama is very bad. If the swelling in her legs and body doesn't go down she probably won't live," one voice said. It was a boy's voice.

Inuwa thought how lucky he was. At least his father was healthy, and if he could see, there was nothing more Inuwa could ask.

74

"I'm sorry, Dokwali. Are you planning to take your mother home then?" said the other voice, a woman's.

"The *dokita* said he would tell me tomorrow if I should take her home. There is another medicine he wants to use. If it doesn't work, then . . ." the boy's voice trailed off.

"Have you been cooking food for your mother, Dokwali?" asked the second voice.

"There is no one else to do it. She wants me with her all the time so that I can't even go out to gather wood. I used my last stick tonight. I don't know what I'll do tomorrow."

Inuwa thought of the big pile of wood he had managed to collect. He had expected to get several shillings by selling it next market day. But he could surely spare a little for this boy who obviously needed it worse than he did. He turned around to speak. He himself was in the shadow, but there was enough light to see the boy's face silhouetted against the light. His hair was braided down the back. It was that Diya boy!

Inuwa turned back around swiftly before the boy saw him. He couldn't help that boy! Not after all the things he had done! Inuwa very quietly but quickly moved away until he was out of sight in the darkness.

Returning to his sleeping house, he lay down on his mat. Saratu was asleep. He stared at the ceiling, waiting for sleep to come. But it would not. What was wrong with him? He usually went right to sleep. He kept hearing the Diya boy saying, "She probably won't live." He turned over on his right side, then his left side. That boy was a thief; he did not deserve sympathy.

Finally he slept, but he dreamed. In one dream he walked to the door of the women's ward and looked inside. His mother lay on a bed just inside, her eyes closed. He turned away, crying.

He sat up suddenly, tears in his eyes. When he realized it was a dream, he pulled up the blankets and lay back down. Apparently he was cold; that was why he had had a nightmare.

A few voices beginning to stir outside told him that it would soon be day. Again he tried to go to sleep, but it was no use.

Finally he threw the blanket aside. He did not have to

dress, for he had slept in his clothes as always. He stood up and wrapped the blanket around himself. Being careful not to waken Saratu, he made his way to the door.

Chapter 11

A CHANCE FOR REVENGE

Just inside the door he felt rather than saw the pile of wood he had collected on his trips into the bush. Stick by stick, noiselessly, he picked up an armload. Then he stepped out into the predawn glow. He could barely see where to walk to avoid stepping on cooking pots and people sleeping outside on the ground.

He walked toward the lean-to rooms. The new grass of which the lean-to mats were woven was shiny even in the dim light. As he neared the room that he knew to be the one, he stopped and looked around carefully. A few people were starting cooking fires. One family was apparently starting for home, leaving early to avoid the heat. They were arranging their belongings in two gourds to be carried on their heads. No one seemed to notice Inuwa.

Suddenly he was afraid. What if someone saw him and thought he was stealing something? He would go lay the wood down quickly and walk away. He did not think there was anyone else in the room with the Diya boy, so he could leave it at the doorway.

He walked quickly to the door, laid down the wood beside the door and turned in one motion. Suddenly from the inside of the house a hand grabbed him. He jerked to free himself, but the grasp was too firm.

A man's voice said gruffly, "What do you think you are doing?"

"I . . . just brought some wood," replied Inuwa, still struggling.

"You wouldn't be trying to escape if you had just brought some wood. And who would bring wood as a gift anyway? I don't believe you."

"It is for . . ." Inuwa could not bring himself to say the name. "For the Diya boy."

"Dokwali? Well, we'll see! Dokwali, come here."

Inuwa struggled again but could not break the grasp.

There was the sound of movement inside the lean-to, and in the now half-light Inuwa saw a figure with a braid down his back emerge. He was yawning. He tripped over a piece of wood but caught himself. He peered down but apparently could not see clearly.

"Looks like it was a good thing you slept in my house last night, Borbor. Someone trying to steal something?" Then as his eyes adjusted, a look of surprise and then anger came over his face. "It's that Munga boy. He . . . he's trying to steal something from me. What did he take?"

"Says he didn't take anything, says he was bringing you some wood."

"That's a lie if I ever heard one," snarled the boy.

Inuwa was angry, very angry. "Just let me take my wood, and I won't bother you again!" He pointed to the pile of wood beside the doorway.

"Hey, where did that come from?" Dokwali asked in surprise.

"I brought it!" said Inuwa in angry disgust. "What a fool I was!"

The boy stared in open-mouthed astonishment. "You . . . you did? But why? How come?"

The man named Borbor broke in. "Guess he thought you needed it. You said you did." The last was more of a question than a statement.

"Yeah, sure, I need it, but . . ."

"But what? Take it and say thanks." Borbor's voice showed irritation.

"Yeah, sure . . . sure. Thanks . . . uh, what's your name?"

"Inuwa," Inuwa said very low.

"Well, thanks, Inuwa," said Borbor with enthusiasm. "Sure was nice of you to share your wood. We know how far you had to walk after it. Don't we, Dokwali?" The question demanded an answer.

"Yeah . . . a long way," stuttered Dokwali.

Inuwa turned without another word and strode away, his back rigid in anger. As he went he heard Borbor say, "What's the matter with you? Couldn't ya even say thanks? You need that wood bad." Inuwa did not hear the reply.

It was light now with the sun just starting above the horizon. He decided to see if his father was awake. He was so angry he had to talk to someone. Only he would not admit what a fool he had been to take the wood, just because he let himself feel sorry for Dokwali's mother.

He walked slowly now, enjoying the cool of the morning. Dawn brought sudden activity. The quiet hum as people began to stir and start their morning food was pleasant, soothing to his fraught nerves. Smoke from a fire rose here and there. He passed several women, babies bundled warmly on their backs, carrying water from the pipe he had seen that first day. He grimaced when he remembered his ignorance.

A small child huddled near his mother's fire, wrapped in a blanket. Another child was crying fitfully where he sat in the doorway of a house. His mother was trying to persuade him to eat a peanut stick, but he just cried.

Inuwa passed through the living-cooking area and started up the walk toward the men's ward. Ahead of him an interesting procession was entering the men's ward. One man carried a mattress rolled up on his head. The next man carried a wooden box with a padlock on it. Behind them came what was obviously an important man. He carried nothing but walked straight and proud. Another man followed, a folding chair balanced perfectly on his head.

Inuwa followed them into the men's ward, wondering who such an important man could be and why he would be coming to the hospital. As he neared the room that was his father's, he saw that they were putting their loads down near his father's bed. The man with the mattress unrolled it and laid it on the empty bed next to his father's. Apparently that patient had left, for someone had been in it yesterday. There were only two beds in each cubicle, but Inuwa was surprised that they would put such an important man in the same room with someone else. The man carrying the box took it off his head and shoved it under the bed. The chair was set up immediately for the man to sit on. The ward attendant came on the run with a sheet for the bed and hurriedly put it on, obviously trying to do an extra good job. They spoke a language Inuwa did not understand, but which he recognized as Diya.

Inuwa slipped as unobtrusively as possible into the space

79

beside his father's bed. Mallam Yaga was awake but still lying on his bed, his bandage-wrapped head turned toward the voices. His bed was steel with springs on which a grass mat was laid, then a sheet just big enough to cover the bed was tied at the four corners to keep it in place.

Inuwa whispered in his father's ear. "*Wana*, Baba. How are you this morning?"

Mallam Yaga returned quietly, "I am feeling even better. Just one more day! Can you tell me what is going on here?"

Inuwa explained briefly in a whisper. He was not sure they could not understand the Munga language, so he took no chances.

"There must not be any private rooms if they would put him here," said his father. "I'm glad to be leaving tomorrow. Being in the same room with someone so important is a strain. Fortunately I can't intrude on his privacy since I can't see. In fact, that is probably why they chose this room to put him in."

All the members of the chief's party ignored Inuwa and his father. Up until then Inuwa had kept his eyes averted as expected. But for just a moment he let his eyes touch the important man's face, and the man smiled at him.

"*Wana*, my son," he said in Munga. "How is your father?"

Inuwa bowed from the waist and replied quickly, "*Wana, Waigana*," which was the title of respect used at such a time. "My father had an operation on his eyes. Tomorrow we will know if he will see again."

The man smiled again. "May God give him sight."

One of the other men stepped forward now and said, "This is Waigana Yusufu, chief of the village of Nasarawa."

Inuwa bowed and returned, "My father is Mallam Yaga Gwonza from Turwa . . . and I am Inuwa."

The chief nodded. "We hear of good things coming from Turwa. Didn't one of your eighth graders score the highest in the secondary school entrance examination last year?"

Inuwa beamed as he assured the chief that this was so.

"What class are you in?" asked the chief.

"I enter class seven this year. I hope to make a high score so I can go on to secondary to be a teacher someday."

"I'm sure you will make it," the chief went on. "A boy who was trusted to accompany his father on such a trip as this must be very capable and very brave. Is that why you are privileged to wear the brass earring?"

Inuwa dropped his gaze. Could the chief read the truth in his eyes? "No . . ." he said hesitantly. "I won it because I am good with the slingshot."

"You are being modest. But that is commendable too."

Inuwa was drawn to this man who did not hate Munga people and who seemed really interested in him.

"May I bring you some water to drink?" asked Inuwa, glancing around for a water container.

One of the men pulled the box from under the bed, opened it and took out a small plastic pail. He said, "Fine. I will go with you to see where to get it."

Inuwa bowed as before and went out, feeling very important.

When he reached their house, Saratu was just dipping guinea corn mush out into an enamel dish. She spooned some of the *panya* on top of the mush and then set the lid of the dish in place.

Inuwa reached for it. "*Kai,* am I hungry!"

"That isn't for you. Maryamu and I have been taking turns cooking for the woman who is in the bed next to Maryamu's mother in the women's ward. Whoever does her cooking does a terrible job. She is so sick and needs food that tastes good. This is for her."

"Where's mine?"

"You can't have yours until I have delivered this to the woman and you have taken your father's food to him."

Inuwa sighed. "All right. Let's get going."

"Walk with me to the women's ward," suggested Saratu.

He was glad for the invitation. He took the covered dish and spoon that Saratu gave him. She carried the other bowl.

As they neared the women's ward, Saratu said, "Go in with me and greet the woman. She never has anyone to visit her."

"I don't want to go in a women's ward!" said Inuwa in alarm. "I'll wait outside."

"Aw, you're silly. Men and boys go in all the time. Some women don't have anyone but a boy to cook for them. But you can wait outside."

81

Inuwa watched as Saratu entered the building. He could see through the windows of each room as she walked down the center aisle and stopped at one of the beds. It was on the side toward him, so he stepped over to the window, standing where he could look in without being seen.

He watched as Saratu took off the bowl lid and held it where the woman could see. But the woman did not look nor did she respond in any way. Saratu spoke to her softly, but there was no answer, no flicker of eyelash. Finally Saratu set the dish down on the bedside stand and covered it. Then she said something to Maryamu's mother in the other bed and walked out, a deep frown on her face.

Just as Inuwa turned to leave, the *dokita* came into the little room. A ward attendant was with him. The *dokita* looked closely at the woman who lay so still. He felt her pulse, laid his hand on her abdomen, listened to her chest and abdomen with the instrument that had two tubes leading to his ears. "She has not responded to any medicine that I have tried. Her body continues to collect fluid instead of getting rid of it. She may already have severe kidney damage." Inuwa listened intently. He was not sure of the meaning of some of the big English words, but it sounded bad for the woman.

Saratu appeared at Inuwa's side. He silenced her with his finger to his lips. She stood out of sight and waited. She understood very little English.

The *dokita* was taking a bottle out of his pocket. He handed it to the attendant. "This is a new medicine that I have not tried. It arrived from America in the mail yesterday. Give her two of these right now and one every three hours the rest of today. Measure the urine output and give me a report at twelve o'clock and again at four." The attendant nodded.

Just then someone greeted the *dokita* as he approached. Inuwa could not see who it was. The *dokita* turned and replied, "Good morning, Dokwali. How are you this morning?"

"Fine, *dokita*. How is my mother?"

"She is not doing at all well, Dokwail. In fact, I am very worried."

Inuwa turned to Saratu. "It's that Diya boy! Did you know you had been bringing food to his mother?"

82

"No!" Saratu almost exploded. Inuwa motioned her to silence and turned back to watch the scene.

Dokwali was speaking in English also. Inuwa had to admit grudgingly that he spoke better English than he did himself. Inuwa hated him even more.

Dokwali's voice dropped, and Inuwa strained to hear. "Then it would be best for me to take her home to Nasarawa?"

"Nasarawa!" Inuwa said to himself. That was the village of the chief in the men's ward.

The *dokita* replied. "Some new medicine arrived yesterday. We are starting her on it immediately. We will know by four o'clock this evening whether or not it will help her. If it does not, then, yes, you should take her home where she may end her time in her own village." The *dokita* spoke kindly. "I'm sorry, Dokwali. She was already very ill when she arrived."

"Yes, I know. My father refused to let her come to the hospital until the medicine *dokita* in our village said there was nothing more he could do for her."

Inuwa was not listening; he was thinking about something else. He still smarted from the rebuff of that morning.

Dokwali was still speaking. "*Dokita*, do you think I could be a nurse when I finish school?"

"There is no reason why not. Being here at the hospital with your mother should have given you a good idea of what it might be like. A nurse must finish secondary school first with good grades, so you must work at that."

Dokwali nodded.

Inuwa, engrossed in his own thoughts, turned away. "Saratu, you go on back to the house. I'll take this to Baba."

"All right, but you'd better hurry. This is your morning for an injection."

"*Kai*! I forgot about that. It seems like I had one just yesterday. All right, I'll get it. You go on."

Saratu left, looking back as if wondering why Inuwa suddenly wanted her to leave. Inuwa started walking around the end of the women's ward. He paused near the door. As he hoped, Dokwali was coming out.

The Diya boy did not see him until Inuwa spoke. Then an expression of fear and anguish came over his face. He

83

stepped back. Inuwa moved toward him. Dokwali took another step back. He opened his mouth as if to speak, but nothing came out.

Inuwa's anger boiled up. "So you steal from us and then call me a thief!" He watched Dokwali's reaction. The boy took another step backward. "Do you know what I'm going to do? I'm going to tell your chief that you stole my wood and our guinea corn." Inuwa paused. Dokwali's face admitted his guilt. "And the meat and tomatoes Saratu bought in market!"

Dokwali's face was contorted. "But!" Nothing else came.

All of Inuwa's pent-up frustration and anger came out. He raised himself up very tall and with an accusing finger pointing at Dokwali, he spoke in a controlled voice, angry, low, but loud enough that Dokwali did not miss a word. "I'm going to tell your chief! Then they will cut off your braid. Your braid that means you are worthy to belong to the tribe. And you will be a disgrace! I'm going to tell your chief!"

Chapter 12

THE END OF THE JOURNEY

Cowering under Inuwa's torrent of words, Dokwali was cornered. With an effort to control his quivering lips, he said, "Okay, so I stole the wood and the guinea corn . . . and the meat and tomatoes, too. But I didn't have any money! Our money was gone and our grain was gone. I had to do something! My mother needed good food to get well!"

He stopped momentarily, looking at Inuwa with pleading eyes. He had regained control of himself, and he raised his voice. "What would you have done? If it had been your mother what would you have done?" Now he was almost shouting. "Haven't you ever done anything wrong? I suppose you've never ever stolen anything or hurt someone or told a lie!"

Abruptly Inuwa turned away. He hated Dokwali, hated him!

Not looking at Dokwali, Inuwa shouted, "But you stole the wood I walked miles into the bush to get and the grain we carried all the way from Turwa! And you the same as lied when I brought the wood this morning."

The brass earring was on the ear turned toward Dokwali. Dokwali's shoulders sagged. "No, a boy who earns a brass earring doesn't do things like that. Yes, they'll cut off my braid." He stood staring at the ground. Then he looked up at Inuwa, pleading. "Don't tell the chief. Please don't!"

Inuwa did not look at Dokwali. He started walking toward the men's ward, the bowl of food in his hand. Dokwali stood staring after him until Inuwa had disappeared into the men's ward.

Inuwa walked quickly until he was inside the ward, then slowed his steps. As he reached his father's room, the chief greeted him. "Welcome, my son. Your father and I have been talking. He is very proud of you, and it sounds as if you are a boy to be proud of."

Inuwa tried to smile. He bowed stiffly and mumbled, "Thank you." His eyes did not meet those of the chief.

The chief continued. "Your father said you have had some trouble with a thief, possibly a Diya boy. Is that true?"

Sweat stood out on Inuwa's forehead, even in the cool of the morning. Here was his chance. Dokwali had no right to take those things! But more than that, he had made him look like a fool this morning. He did not like being made a fool of. Inuwa opened his mouth, but suddenly it was dry, and suddenly the brass ring in his ear was huge and heavy, so heavy that it pulled his head down. He himself had lied! What if his own chief found that out? His mouth was so dry he could hardly speak.

He forced his mouth to say, "We . . . I'm not sure. No, maybe it was someone else."

"Well, I certainly hope so. But if you find out and it is a Diya boy, you tell me, will you? That is a grave offense for a young boy in our tribe."

Inuwa nodded and straightened his head. The earring was light again.

As soon as his father had finished eating, Inuwa hurried out. He was miserable. And having to have an injection did not make him feel any better. The line was very long, and he was at the very end. This time the needle was not sharp. It stung when the man injected the medicine, and it went on stinging for a long time. It was in his hip, which made every movement uncomfortable. Nor could he sit without pain. Finally he lay down on a grass mat in the shade of their house.

He would have liked to sleep, but his thoughts ran in circles, always back to the same one. He had thought that by leaving Turwa he could escape the lie he had told. Instead it seemed to follow his steps and emerge at the most exasperating moments. But right was on his side; that Diya boy had stolen, not once, but many times, and he had the same as lied. He deserved to have his braid cut.

"Dokwali!" He could say the name now, and he hated Dokwali. He hated him because he had made a fool of him . . . and . . . His thoughts returned again to the scene by the women's ward. He hated him most for reminding him of his own lie. He would tell the chief yet! Dokwali never did say he was sorry, nor really admit that he should not have done what he did. Dokwali should come and apologize, at least for the way he treated Inuwa that morning.

And Inuwa's own guilt? Inuwa buried his face in his hands. His hip throbbed as he moved. A ray of sun found its way through the leaves. It felt good, but it did not relieve the pain.

Dokwali's mother was dying. Inuwa's own reason for lying was completely selfish. Dokwali was a coward; but so was he. And each would have to hide his guilt. Each would be alone with it, terribly alone, for they could confide in no one.

Enough! Inuwa jumped up, aching hip and all. He would push those thoughts out of his mind. They would go home day after tomorrow, and he would forget Dokwali and everything that had happened. Home! Back to Tursinda! And? No, he would not let the thought of that enter his mind either. He would worry about that after he got home.

His eyes looked up the main street that led to the path for home. And the journey home? He reached down and picked up his sling. Could anything happen worse than what had already happened on the journey to Birni? He had managed to come out on top each time. The actual thing had not been as bad as his fear of it. He spoke aloud, "I won't be afraid this time. I *won't* be afraid."

"Inuwa, is that you?" It was Saratu's voice. "I've been looking for you."

He came around the house. Saratu was starting a fire. "I've been lying down. My hip is really sore where he gave me my injection."

"That's too bad. I guess I've been lucky. None of mine has hurt."

Inuwa stood and watched Saratu breaking up small twigs. When they were ready, she laid them on the coals which she had borrowed from a neighbor's fire. Then she leaned over and blew until a tiny tongue of flame appeared. Quickly other flames sprang up. She laid on large pieces of wood.

"Are you going to be ready to leave day after tomorrow, Saratu?"

Saratu was tending her cooking fire

"My last injection was yesterday," she replied with a nod. And leaning over, she deftly untied the white bandage on her leg and pulled it off. "See!" she said triumphantly. Nothing remained of the open sore now but a tiny spot. "I am to take some of the medicine home with me and soak my leg until the sore is entirely gone."

"It is a good thing you caught it in time. Bitrus wasn't so lucky."

Saratu nodded. "And the nurse told me how to keep it from happening again. Whenever a bite or cut gets infected, I am to immediately wrap it with a clean cloth, and he told me how to prepare cloths so they are absolutely clean and to store them until I need them." Saratu spoke excitedly. "And you know, I can tell my friends who get ulcers how to take care of them!"

Inuwa smiled approval. "That'll be great! Lots of people in Turwa have ulcers." He thought about that a moment. "I'll be glad to get back to Turwa. I'm anxious to be on the way."

"So am I," agreed Saratu. "I'm getting tired of cooking two meals a day every day."

"Really?" asked Inuwa, looking surprised. "I supposed anyone who cooks as well as you do would never get tired of doing it."

That flustered Saratu so that she dropped the piece of wood she was putting on the fire. She ducked her head and quickly began pulling the scattered fire back into the center. Inuwa grinned to himself. Suddenly Saratu stood up. She reached into her pocket and pulled out something which she thrust toward him.

"This is for you," she said awkwardly, not looking at him. Quickly she turned away, grabbed the water bucket and headed off toward the water pipe. Inuwa unfolded the piece of white cloth. It was a hand-hemmed handkerchief. She had obviously done it herself. He folded it carefully and stuck it in the waist of his trousers. Then he took off at a run to catch up with her.

After carrying the water for Saratu, Inuwa walked down the road to the little canteen, the store where candies, matches and other items were available between market days. He needed to buy a headscarf for Ladi. At his father's instructions he had bought lengths of cloth in the market for his mother and Mama Wani, but he still had to find something for his sister. As he was waiting for his change, he noticed a small clock on a shelf that showed the time to be almost four o'clock. He wondered what report was being given on Dokwali's mother.

When he returned to the house, food was ready. Saratu was dipping up the guinea corn mush for Mallam Yaga.

"Are you taking food to Dokwali's mother tonight?" asked Inuwa.

"It is Maryamu's turn."

"Did you tell her about . . ." He left the sentence dangling.

"Yes, but she said she wouldn't stop taking it because the woman was so sick and needed good food. So I guess I'll go on doing it too."

"While I take food to Baba, why don't you go up and see how she is?" He spoke offhandedly as if he didn't really care.

Saratu nodded. She handed the dish she had filled to Inuwa and started off toward the women's ward immediately.

Inuwa was glad his father was sitting outside, so he did not have to meet the chief.

When Inuwa returned from the men's ward, Saratu came to meet him. "Inuwa! You wouldn't believe it! That woman is sitting up, laughing and talking. She ate every bit of what Maryamu took to her. Isn't that wonderful!"

A strong feeling of relief came over Inuwa. He had not realized how much he wanted Dokwali's mother to get better.

"It is wonderful, isn't it, Inuwa?" Saratu asked, searching his face anxiously.

"Yes, Saratu, it's wonderful. Now if only Baba can see. Tomorrow we find out."

Inuwa's hip still ached when he lay down on his mat to go to sleep. But it was not that which kept him awake. What was he going to do about Dokwali? He had left Dokwali with the impression that he was going to tell the chief. Well, he didn't do it, did he? Did he have to do anything else? Dokwali would go on worrying and wondering. So? He deserved to worry a little. But didn't Dokwali have enough on his mind with his mother so sick? His mother was much better now. Inuwa turned over resolutely. As far as he was concerned, the matter was finished.

Of all mornings, Inuwa slept later than usual the next morning.

"Inuwa, this is the day! Have you forgotten?" Saratu said from the doorway.

Inuwa leaped up from his mat and dashed outside. He splashed a little water on his face. With a quick greeting to Saratu he raced off toward the men's ward. As he stepped hurriedly into the doorway, he almost collided with a man coming out.

"Inuwa! Inuwa! I can see you!" His father went on out the door, looking eagerly in one direction and then another. "I can see the tree, and the benches, and the compounds over there!"

"Baba, that's wonderful! Wonderful, wonderful, wonderful!" And Inuwa danced around his father.

The *dokita* stood there smiling as did the hospital attendants and other patients attracted by the excitement. Even the chief had come to watch. He was smiling. Beside him stood a boy. It was Dokwali. Anger welled up inside Inuwa that Dokwali should be allowed to participate in their moment of joy.

They began moving back into the men's ward except for Mallam Yaga and the *dokita* who stood outside talking. Inuwa started picking up the items belonging to his father. He had noted that Dokwali returned reluctantly with the chief and was now kneeling beside the chief's chair.

Waigana Yusufu called to Inuwa. "Inuwa, I want you to meet another son of mine. This is Dokwali, from my own village. We in Nasarawa are very proud of Dokwali. He has stayed here with his mother for many weeks, looking after her, cooking food. You know how boys dislike cooking food."

Inuwa nodded. He looked at the unsmiling Dokwali, and suddenly he understood. Dokwali was miserable. He dared not look directly at the chief for fear his guilt would show in his eyes, and the chief would know the awful things he had done. Inuwa had felt this same thing over and over. And now Dokwali would have to live with his guilt. Yet he had done a courageous thing, to cook and care for his mother with no one to help him. How lonely he must have been in his grief and guilt.

Suddenly Inuwa reached up and pulled the brass earring from his ear. He extended his hand, palm up with the shiny ring in it.

"I . . . I don't deserve this," he said.

The chief was surprised. "Oh, but . . ." he began.

"No, no, I don't deserve it. I cheated on part of the test . . . because I was afraid."

The chief said nothing, seemed to be waiting for him to go on.

And at last, Inuwa could look someone in the eye. The relief was so great that his words tumbled out.

"I was afraid to sleep out in the bush, so I sneaked back into the village until dawn. I didn't think I would win . . . not this year . . . maybe next year. Then when I did, I couldn't admit that I had cheated. I just thought no one would ever know."

Inuwa's eyes clung to those of the chief, pleading. Waigana Yusufu gazed at him a long moment after Inuwa's voice trailed off. Slowly he put out his hand and took the earring.

"Inuwa, you have done the right thing, and the courageous thing. In all probability no one would ever have known."

Inuwa interrupted, "But I knew, and . . ."

Waigana Yusufu nodded solemnly, "And you are the one you have to live with the rest of your life." The chief was silent a moment. "Waigana Yamta of Turwa is my friend. I will send this earring to him with an explanation. No, better yet, I will write a letter to him, and you take it to him."

Inuwa drew back, fear in his eyes again.

"You have nothing to fear now, Inuwa. You have shown great courage in the way you took care of your father and Saratu on the journey to Birni. And it has required much courage to admit your guilt. The hardest part is over, but it is your chief who has the power to forgive you. And I know Waigana Yamta to be understanding." He stopped speaking and waited for Inuwa's response. There were no words, but the fear slowly left Inuwa's eyes. He nodded.

"I will prepare the letter and give it to your father."

Inuwa drew in a quick breath. "Oh, no!" he said before he could catch himself. His father! He could bear for anyone else to know . . . except his father, who never could lie, or cheat or be afraid. He couldn't . . .

He turned away, frantic, trapped in an impossible situation. He would leave, run out of there.

But as he turned, he found himself facing his father.

From behind him came the voice of the chief, kindly but firmly, "Tell him, Inuwa."

Inuwa stood for a long moment, his insides shriveling up as he looked into his father's eyes. Finally he took a long breath and began. "Baba, I . . . cheated in the trials. I didn't really deserve the brass ring. I'm sorry, Baba." His voice broke, and he turned to flee.

But his father reached out and put his hand on Inuwa's arm. "I know, son, I've known since the day before we left for our journey. The boy who saw you returning to the bush came to me. I have just been waiting for you to tell me."

"But I couldn't tell you!" cried Inuwa. "You are never afraid. And . . ."

"Inuwa, let me tell you something. Do you remember when you left me alone to go back after the water bottle? I was terrified. That night in the bush I only pretended to sleep because I was so afraid. It was your strength and your skill that finally brought us to Birni. You even stood off the mad dog!"

"But I was so scared!"

"Of course, you were. But there is nothing wrong with being afraid; it is what you do with your fear that is important. You showed over and over that you could conquer fear."

Inuwa stood there, trying to comprehend what his father had just said.

The chief came and stood beside Inuwa, his arm across his shoulders. He held out the brass ring.

"Take this to Waigana Yamta, Inuwa, and tell him the story . . . the whole story."

Inuwa took the earring, gripping it tightly in his fist. He wanted to get away, to think about what had happened so quickly. He gave a low bow and started moving away, saying, "*Wana*, Waigana," softly.

Dokwali put out his hand as if to stop Inuwa. "You didn't tell him . . ." he faltered.

Inuwa shook his head. "I couldn't. You tell him; he will understand."

Inuwa picked up his father's belongings, bowed again and turned to leave.

Waigana Yusufu called after him, "Go in peace, Inuwa, and with a smiling heart."

As they rounded the last curve, the smoke from cooking fires rose straight up in the still evening. They peered ahead eagerly. Their steps quickened. Then a small figure appeared in the doorway with an animal beside it. The two travelers waved. The animal raised its head and sniffed. The girl pointed, then turned to call to someone within the compound.

A cry carried through the twilight, "Tursinda!"

Two shapes, one a half-grown dog and the other a half-grown boy, raced toward each other in the gathering dusk. And the man walked proudly up the path by himself.

A GLOSSARY OF WORDS

"Aiya"	an exclamation
Baba	Father
banza	no good, worthless
danjiki	boy's shirt
dokita	doctor
gapani	no good, worthless
harmattan	fine dust which sifts down from the Sahara desert
"I'I"	Yes
"Kai"	an exclamation
Kaka	Grandmother
katanga	a small deadly snake
kobo	one-cent piece
krola	soft drink
"Lalay"	"Welcome"
lorry	truck
luptu	girl's short dress or blouse
mbula	a kind of tree having thick shade
mindi	meningitis
panya	food made by mixing meat and vegetables
"Salaam aleakum"	"Peace to you"
schistosomiasis	a tropical disease, also known as bladder worm disease, or Bilharzia
Waigana	a title of respect
"Wana"	an exclamation or greeting
zhebi	cloth to wrap around as a skirt or shawl